ON THE ROAD TO NOWHERE.

Less than twenty feet ahead of me, a cluster of weirdly flickering lights wavered across the road like giant fireflies in the woods, except we don't have fireflies here. Not flashlights, the light was too yellow. And were those people? Vague shadows, and I couldn't tell if they were moving or not.

My gut made me slam on the brakes even though I knew better. Not that it did any good. The Crown Vic squirted across the mud as if I'd hit the gas instead. I heard someone scream, even through the rolled-up windows. I steered into the skid trying to regain control, but I might as well have yanked the steering wheel loose for all the good it did me.

The very last thing I remember was seeing one of those damned orange larches careening through the windshield straight at me.

Books by M.M. Justus

Tales of the Unearthly Northwest

Sojourn

"New Year's Eve in Conconully"

Reunion

Time in Yellowstone

Repeating History

True Gold

"Homesick"

Finding Home

Much Ado in Montana

Cross-Country: Adventures Alone Across America and Back

SOJOURN

THE FIRST TALE OF THE UNEARTHLY NORTHWEST

M.M. JUSTUS

Carbon
River
Press

Sojourn

Second print edition published by 2014 Carbon River Press
Copyright © 2014 M.M. Justus
Cover art copyright © Can Stock Photo Inc. / johnnorth
and © Can Stock Photo Inc. / eunika
Cover design copyright © 2014 M.M. Justus
978-1503146327

Carbon River Press
http://carbonriverpress.com

)

ACKNOWLEDGEMENTS

Thank you to the real towns of Conconully and Molson, Washington, and to the Okanogan County Historical Society, for the historical markers and the inspiration.

To Elizabeth Stowe for beta reading and many useful conversations.

And to Elizabeth McCoy for her always perceptive editing, as well as for pointing out where Dan grabbed the idiot ball along with excellent suggestions for taking it away from him again.

SOJOURN

Chapter 1

The bizarre old truck literally came flying out of nowhere. I'd been on my way back from a car fire out near Chesaw and, at first glimpse, I thought it was another fire engine. It was red, all right, but that pickup was older than I was, and all I could see of the driver was a glint of silver as the heap screamed past me at suicide-by-car-wreck speeds.

My vehicle, a standard-issue Washington State Highway Patrol Crown Victoria, rocked in its wake. The road wasn't wide enough to make a U, with a ditch on either side. I wasted the better part of half a mile trying to find a spot to swing the cruiser around. I slapped the lights and siren on then, and gave chase.

Not that the driver was going to get far at the rate she was going. I braced myself for carnage around every bend in the narrow two-lane mountain road, but each time I came around a curve the road was empty. The Okanogan Highlands in early November are desolate enough as it is, and I didn't have time to think about it as I almost skidded around the curves as fast as the Crown Vic would let me, but when I thought back on it later, it seemed odd how I didn't wonder why I saw no one else out there just before sundown that day.

At the time all I could think was, what the hell and why and who *is* that stupid idiot and please God don't let me find a pile of twisted metal upside down in a ditch.

I must have gone at least five miles, and was about to give up completely when I caught another glimpse of red through the trees. It was as if she'd been waiting for me to catch up, because no sooner did I see the truck than she took off again. A metallic "nyah, nyah, can't catch me" all but bounced through my brain, and I slammed my foot on the gas.

Damned drysiders. Nobody'd told me when the Washington State Patrol assigned me to the biggest, least populated county in the state that the few people who lived here had gone completely psycho from too much wide open space. An oversight, I'm sure.

I lost and found that truck at least three more times before she slammed on its brakes and careened off the highway about a quarter mile ahead of me. I could see the fishtailed tread marks as I reached the spot a few seconds later, but damned if I saw anything resembling a road for her to have turned off onto.

You're probably wondering why I keep referring to the driver as her, when statistically that kind of daredevil is male and the only thing I could have said for sure just then was whoever it was had gray hair. I'm only going to say I had my reasons. I'm not sure what they were, but I remember having them. And whatever my half-cocked reasoning was at the time, it turned out to be right.

I pulled over and turned off the siren, but left the lights on, since the shoulder really wasn't wide enough to park the car on and the road was curvy enough to block the view from more than a few yards in either direction. I didn't relish the idea of having to explain getting my cruiser rear-ended while it was parked out in the middle of nowhere.

I got out and inspected the skid marks: impressive, perfect half-moon curves. When I followed them to the edge of the road, I could see the dry, golden grass was flattened, and smell the dusty juices. Something of a track went further on past the shoulder. I gazed up and around at the gray sky and dull gold hills. I had no idea where I was – well, I was somewhere south of Chesaw and if I stayed on the paved road I'd probably end up back in Tonasket on Highway 97. Eventually. But this part of the Okanogan Highlands is laced with dirt roads leading to nowhere. Or to holes in the ground, with a few decaying shacks standing guard around them. This was gold mining country a hundred years ago.

A glint of red caught my eye again, disappearing behind a clump of orange larches further on up the hill. There's nothing weirder than a conifer that turns color and loses its, well, not leaves, obviously, but goes naked in the winter like a damned maple.

It was the principle of the thing by now. Sighing, hoping I didn't live to regret my decision, I climbed back in the cruiser and edged it carefully off the pavement. I didn't want to think how I was going to explain this to Sergeant MacKade if I had to call in and get a tow truck out here. If I could get any kind of cell phone or radio reception out here in the first place.

I had to give the idiot in the red truck credit. The track widened a couple hundred yards off the highway into a real, live dirt road. It was almost as if whoever lived back off up here didn't want the world to know it existed. After a while, as the Vic crept up the track, dust dampened out of existence from the front that had dropped a stingy few drops the night before, I began to relax, almost against my will.

It wasn't as if I could go any faster, not without risking damage to the cruiser. I knew my quarry couldn't go any faster, either. She couldn't be going that far. Probably to one of those big lone houses on the hilltops overlooking the valley and the apple orchards below. The sergeant had warned me about some of the people who lived in them when I'd first arrived back in August, fresh from the academy. Fresh from getting dumped by Linda, too, because I'd been assigned to the back of beyond, even though it wasn't my fault. It wasn't like I'd had a choice. It was either come here or waste two years of academy training.

I stopped that train of thought before it could get away from me again. It had too many times before, and I needed to figure out how I was going to handle this situation when I got there.

The kind of rich people who live out here are here because they don't want a lot of government interfering in their lives. Well, I was going to interfere this time, if only because the rest of the county didn't deserve some maniac driving under the influence and putting one of them into the hospital. Or worse.

The road, such as it was, reached the top of the hill, but the big fancy house, lording it over a view that probably was pretty darned spectacular in clear weather, wasn't there. No buildings in sight, as a matter of fact. Just two ruts, separated by a line of grass, meandering down the other side of the hill back into the green and orange woods.

This was getting ridiculous. I debated turning around and heading back to town. Daylight was all but gone, the clouds were sinking like someone was pushing down on them from above, and it was going to take me the better part of two hours to get back to Omak, sign out for the day, and go home.

To my empty apartment, to do what on a Saturday night? Nobody wants to party with the new state trooper in town. If there was one thing I'd learned about small towns, it was that if you weren't living in the house your grandparents were born in, you might as well have the word "outsider" printed across your forehead with a magic marker. The cop thing just made it worse.

What the hell. It wasn't like I had anything else to do. I kept going.

Over the river and through the damned woods. Well, except there wasn't a river. There was a creek – excuse me, that's a "crick" on the dry side of the Cascades – with a grove of white-trunked and leafless aspens between it and the road. Lots of forest, though – pines so green they were almost black and the larches standing out against them like torches in the dark. I turned the flashers off, leaving the steady, solid headlights on. The last thing I needed was some sort of strobe illusion making me think I was seeing something that wasn't there.

The rain started up again, more than a few drops this time, making silver lines in the high beams and blurring the windshield. I cursed and flipped the wipers on, and would have turned around then, DUI or no DUI, if there'd been a space wide enough to maneuver the car. But there wasn't. Even if there had been, the hillside I'd been creeping along for the last five minutes or so seemed to drop into some sort of black hole of a canyon to my right, and I didn't want to take the chance of sliding the cruiser off into it, never to be found again. Even if no one would miss me if I did. Not Linda, for damned sure. Not Dad and Carol, either. Dad hadn't missed me for years, and I'd long since finished being Carol's responsibility, thank God. Not anyone.

Why was I on this road to nowhere again?

Right. I was trying to catch a probable crazy person who'd most likely already skidded off into the canyon herself. The dirt under my tires was turning into something resembling a slip 'n slide, and the track was getting narrower and narrower, and more and more overgrown, although I wasn't sure that wasn't just my paranoia making me think so.

I could have reached out and touched the barren rocky hillside through the driver's side window, and on my right the cliff dropped away into darkness. Someone'd had a heck of a time blasting this road out of the hill. I edged around yet another curve, hoping for a spot wide enough to turn around and go, well, if not home, then at least back to Omak.

Less than twenty feet ahead of me, a cluster of weirdly flickering lights wavered across the road like giant fireflies in the woods, except we don't have fireflies here. Not flashlights, the light was too yellow. And were those *people*? Vague shadows, and I couldn't tell if they were moving or not. My gut made me slam on the brakes even though I knew better. Not that it did any good. The Vic squirted across the mud as if I'd hit the gas instead. I heard someone scream, even through the rolled-up windows. I steered into the skid trying to regain control, but I might as well have yanked the steering wheel loose for all the good it did me.

The very last thing I remember was seeing one of those damned orange larches careening through the windshield straight at me.

CHAPTER 2

The voices came at me from a long way off at first. Lots of voices, all different, male and female, old and young. All saying the same thing, and getting louder and closer with each anxious question.

"Doc Amy?"

"Doc Amy? Is he all right?"

"Doc Amy? How bad is he hurt?"

"Is he going to die, Doc Amy?"

That one got my attention, in spite of my head feeling like somebody'd hit it with a two by four. Be careful what you wish for, was all I could think. Not that I'd really wanted to die. Not right then, and not like that, at any rate.

"No, he's not going to die, you fool." Or maybe not, since it apparently hadn't worked. Maybe I hadn't asked directly enough. Or hadn't had the guts to. But the voice, young and female, made me – I wouldn't go so far as to say *glad*, but still – I hadn't died. And she sounded like she knew what she was talking about. Reassuring. In charge. So maybe I had a second chance. I was vaguely surprised to realize I wanted one. "Go on, all of you. Get out. Now."

A sound of shuffling, like shoes on a wooden floor, and abruptly the room became much more quiet. The room? Apparently. And, yes, a bed. A very soft, very comfortable bed, now that I noticed it. Not at all like the rock of a mattress in my furnished apartment in Omak.

"I know you're in there, darn you. Wake up before I shake you." Her voice sounded angry. "I'm going to murder Audrey for this. She had no right –" A warm damp cloth swiped gently at my face. A sweet scent reached my nose. I felt like I should know that scent, but I couldn't place it.

I was trying, honest I was, but somehow I just knew if I opened my eyes my head was going to fall off and roll across the floor, and I was pretty sure I needed it to stay on my shoulders.

"You're not hurt that bad. You can't be. You weren't going fast enough to hurt yourself that bad."

"Fast," I said. Or tried to say. She didn't answer, so maybe she couldn't hear me. I wanted to reach up and hold my head, keep it from falling off, but then a pair of hands did it for me. Small hands, but strong, holding my head steady and still. I took a breath to try again, but she beat me to it.

"Don't jerk yourself around like that. I'm pretty sure you didn't do any damage to your neck or your spine, but I'd just as soon not find out the hard way." The hands tightened, just a bit. Secure. Good.

"Thank you."

"What?!" The hands flinched against my skin, but held steady. "Did you just say what I thought you said?"

I tried again. It came out louder this time. "Thank you."

"Oh, my gosh. Oh, my gosh." Her tone changed utterly. I could hear her breathing now, almost gasping. "You're alive. Okay, I knew you were alive, but I mean you're really alive, not just lying there doing nothing but breathing." She was talking really, really fast now, but her hands still held me like a rock. "Oh, gosh. Okay, okay. Can you open your eyes for me? Please? I'd give anything if you'd just open your eyes."

She didn't know how much she was asking for, but I'd have given her just about anything right then, she seemed to want it so badly. To want something from *me*, even if all she wanted was for me to be alive. It was more than anyone else had wanted in a long time. I took a deep breath, and pushed as hard as I could to get my eyes open.

The first thing I saw was her eyes, so close I could see the wide black pupils in pools of bright blue. Beautiful eyes, surrounded by golden yellow lashes, in the dark room lit only by a pale glow coming from beside us. They widened even further as I watched, mesmerized.

"Omigosh, omigosh, omigosh," she chanted. Then, loudly enough to bounce off the inside of my skull, "Audrey, you numskull, you *didn't* kill him!"

Another voice at the door; not one of the others; it sounded older somehow. "I know that, Amy dear." I had a mental flash of silver hair in a red truck, the one that had gotten me into this mess. Was this Audrey the culprit? If so, I was in no shape to do anything about it. One of – Amy's? – hands loosened its grip and her thumb smoothed across my forehead. I wished she'd do it again, but I didn't want to interrupt to ask.

"No, you didn't." Her blue eyes never left my face.

"You have no faith, dear." The voice sounded amused.

"Maybe not, but that's beside the point. Did you get the liniment? Set it here where I can reach it."

"Yes, here it is." Amy – Doc Amy? – settled back, her hands slipping away from me.

"Hold. Head." It was going to fall off if she didn't, I just knew it. Besides, my skin felt cold where her hands had been. I gritted my teeth against the throbbing, which I'd managed to forget for a few precious minutes.

The older woman – Audrey – chuckled.

"Please go get some more cloths for me," Amy said. She sounded exasperated.

I heard footsteps leaving the room, but Amy didn't put her hands back on my head. Instead she disappeared from my field of vision for a moment, then came back with another damp cloth. This one smelled sharply of something herbal. She put it on my forehead, right over the place where the throbbing came from. How did she know?

I probably had a lump there the size of my fist. It sure felt like it, but it didn't matter. The throbbing backed off, just a little. I closed my eyes again, suddenly exhausted.

"Wore you out, did I?" Her exasperation had faded into amusement. The cloth came and went, along with her small, strong hands. My head began to feel a bit more like it was going to stay fastened to my neck. I gave up, and let myself fall back into the darkness of wherever I'd been.

* * *

The next time I woke up was because I was starving to death and something smelled fantastic. I opened my eyes and promptly closed them again. The candle was gone. The window, which I hadn't even realized existed last night, had its curtains thrown wide open, and the sun was bright enough to scald me to the very backs of my eyeballs.

"Oh, no, you don't," said Doc Amy. Whatever it was that smelled so good came closer, and it wasn't just the food or the herbal stuff. I think it was her. "Open your eyes again and I'll give you some of Audrey's soup. She's the best cook in town, and that's saying something."

"Bright," I said, hoping she'd get the point.

"What? Oh." The bowl went down on the table with a soft thump and a moment later I could hear fabric swish. I opened my eyes again, a bit more cautiously, but the curtain was closed and the light wasn't quite so blinding. "That better?"

"Yes. Thank you."

She smiled. "You're quite the gentleman, aren't you? No, here, let me help you sit up. You shouldn't be jolting yourself around like that."

I had to agree with her, even though I didn't like it much. I let her prop me up with pillows and got my first good look at my doctor.

She was tiny. I wouldn't believe she was five feet tall without proof. She had pale blonde hair drawn back in a messy ponytail draping halfway down her back, the blue eyes I'd seen before now full of mischief, and pink cheeks from the exertion of manhandling me. She sat down in the straight chair beside my bed and picked up the bowl. "You're in for a treat. Audrey's minestrone is to die for. Although I'm glad you didn't." Her smile widened and she held up a spoonful.

I reached for the spoon, only to realize for the first time that my right hand was bandaged. I tried to lift it and decided that was a bad idea. "How?"

She shook her head. I don't know if she misunderstood me, or didn't want to answer me. "Just open up. I'll make sure it ends up in your mouth and not down your front."

Hunger won out over curiosity, and like a little kid, I opened my mouth and let her feed me. I felt like I hadn't eaten in days. She was right about whoever this Audrey person was and her ability to cook. The soup was incredible, rich and delicious.

Amy kept spooning it down me until the bowl was empty, and even wiped my mouth for me. I shook my head again, then waited for all the loose pieces to settle back into place. I was making a hell of an impression. Not that it mattered. Not that I could do anything about it, either.

"You're still hurting, aren't you? Well, after the bang-up you went through, I'm not surprised. I wish I had something stronger to give you for it, but I think we can risk some willow bark now that you've got something in your stomach."

She reached over to the small table and set the bowl down, then picked up a cup full of dark liquid that didn't smell so good.

Her smile turned wry. Even through the pain in my head and knowing her expression was an apology for wanting me to drink that stuff, her smile made my breath catch. She didn't look old enough to be anyone's doctor, and she was way too pretty for the job.

She brought the cup to my lips. The liquid touched them, and I touched my tongue to it. "Ugh," I told her, pulling back. "Disgusting."

"Yes, I know. Drink it anyway. It's better than nothing for the pain."

"Aspirin?" I asked hopefully, but she shook her head.

"Sort of. Same active ingredient, anyway." She brought the cup to my lips again and tilted it slightly. "Open up. Get it over with and I'll give you a peppermint to chase it."

Great. She really did think I was a kid. I took a breath, gave her a dirty look, which she responded to with a shrug, and opened my mouth.

God, that stuff was evil. I don't even begin to know how to describe it.

Amy laughed. "You should see your face." She unwrapped the peppermint she'd promised and I reached for it with my left hand. I managed to get it to my mouth without dropping it, and let the mint explode over my tongue.

"That better?"

"Yeah," I mumbled around the candy.

"I think you've had enough excitement for now. Let's get you back down."

After I was horizontal again, I watched her as she puttered around the room, gathering dishes and clothes. At last she turned to me. "I need to get some more arnica for your bump. You just rest." She chuckled. "And if you're good I'll bring you another peppermint."

I was still trying to think of something to say to *that* when she left the room.

* * *

She hadn't been gone long when another head poked around the door. This one was much older and grayer. And taller. And familiar, somehow. As if I should have known her, but didn't. Audrey?

She didn't come in. As a matter of fact, as soon as she noticed I was awake, before I could say her name, her eyes popped wide and she disappeared.

The next thing I knew, the window was full of faces. I couldn't see them clearly through the lace curtain, but their eyes were as wide as Audrey's and they shuffled and bumped for room at the glass as if I was the strangest thing they'd ever seen. I dragged the covers up with my good hand, wishing for thicker curtains. One of them knocked against the window frame just as Amy came back into the room. She sighed and set down the bottle and cloth she was carrying.

"Just a minute, while I chase the gawkers off again."

"Wait." I don't know why I said that. "Again?" And managed a complete sentence. "Why are they staring at me?"

She shrugged. "You're a stranger. We don't get many new faces in town." She went to the window, threw back the curtains and shoved the sash up, but in the few seconds it took her to do it, the crowd had scattered. She pulled the window back down and twitched the curtain back into place.

"Where am I?" God knows it had taken me long enough to realize I had questions to ask, but suddenly I was boiling with them. "What happened to me? Where's my car? Where's my radio? I need my phone."

"Shh..." She came back over to the bed and sat down. "It's not good for you to be agitated while you're recovering from a concussion."

She was probably right. My head was pounding again, but at that point it was the least of my worries. "I won't be agitated if you answer my questions." You'd think that would be obvious.

She looked me over, then sat silently, as if trying to figure out what to say. I didn't want her figuring out what to say. I just wanted her to tell me. I repeated the one question that mattered the most. "Where am I?"

"What do you remember?"

"Oh, no." She wasn't going to get away with that one. What was she, a damned defense lawyer? "*You* tell *me*."

A voice came from out in the hall. "Doc Amy?"

She stood. I reached for her with my left hand, but she slipped away from me. She looked – relieved? Why, dammit? "Yes, Audrey, I'll be right there." She looked down at me with, was that regret in her eyes? Regret for what? She'd saved my life. "I'm sorry. I'll be back in a bit."

"Wait a minute."

"I'm sorry, I can't." And she was out the door and gone. Again.

I had to get out of this damned bed. I lifted the covers with my left hand, and realized for the first time that I was almost naked. Someone – *who?* – had undressed me down to my t-shirt and briefs. I could see my uniform, in a neatly-folded pile on the dresser across the room, my boots lined up side by side next to it. I had to get dressed, get out of this room, find out what was going on, get hold of my phone, call the station, find out what happened to the cruiser.

I couldn't remember anything after that tree looming closer and closer, the Vic sliding down the hill...

After that, everything was a blank. Till I woke up here. Surely that pipsqueak of a doctor, who didn't look old enough to be a doctor, hadn't pulled me out of the car all by her lonesome.

Obviously, at least some of those gawkers, as she'd called them, had helped. They had to know as much as she did.

I sat up and swung my feet around, and nearly passed out as the world swayed around me like I was on the swing ride at the Puyallup Fair. I grabbed the edge of the little table to keep from falling over, and nearly knocked both it and me to the floor.

"What are you *doing*, you young fool?" This voice was appalled, baritone, and belonged to a steel-haired man in a flannel shirt, jeans, and boots standing in the doorway. Despite the hair, he wasn't someone I'd have wanted to take on in a fight even before the accident.

He strode into the room, over to me, and pushed me unceremoniously, if gently, back down into the bed. He swung my feet back up for me before I could do it myself, and in a few swift motions tucked the covers so tightly around me that I couldn't have moved if I'd tried.

"And stay there," he thundered, turned, and strode right back out before I could say anything.

I lay still. My head was churning, my brain sloshing about in its casing as if someone had stirred it to mush. I couldn't move. I was a prisoner. How was I supposed to escape?

* * *

After a bit, as the pounding in my head began to recede slightly, other aches began to make themselves known. I tried to ignore them as I worked my shoulders free of the covers that probably weren't tight enough to choke me even if they felt like they were. I had just managed to get my good hand free when Amy showed back up.

She immediately came over and yanked the covers loose. "I'm sorry. Rob tends to take his duties a bit too seriously."

"What are his duties? Keeping me prisoner? Are you going to tell me where the hell I am or not?"

She looked at me as if I'd let loose with a whole string of profanities a lot worse than one simple hell. The disapproval fairly shimmered off her. Funny, I wouldn't have pegged her for a prude, and maybe I'd misled her when I first woke up, but I hadn't been clearheaded enough to be angry then.

When she didn't stop glaring at me, I said, "Excuse my French. But I think I've got more right to be pis– ticked at you than you do at me right now."

She still looked like she had a stick up her butt. "I apologized for Rob's behavior."

"I couldn't care less about that. Why won't you tell me where the–" at this point I couldn't have thought of a profanity strong enough, anyway "–where I *am*?"

Her expression faded from annoyance to frustration. Frustration? "Because I don't know."

That was the last thing I'd expected her to say. "You don't *know?*"

She looked to the ceiling as if she'd find the answers I wanted written there. After all this time flat on my back, I could tell her they weren't. After a moment, she brought her gaze back to me. "No." After another moment, she said, "I can tell you what happened to you last night, if it's any consolation."

It was a start. If I could just get her talking, I'd get the rest of it out of her. How could she not know where we were? "Go on."

"You ran your police car off the road." She hesitated.

"I figured that much."

"The car is totaled, I'm afraid. You were going far too fast for the conditions and the slope is steep and rocky. Audrey says–" She stopped again.

I prompted her. "What does Audrey say?"

"Audrey said you were driving as if you didn't care if you lived or died."

"I was *chasing* someone who obviously didn't care if – *was* that your Audrey? What was her problem? Didn't she know she could have killed herself? Or somebody else?" Focus, Reilly, I thought. "Never mind. Go on."

"It took a while to get you out of the car." Her baby blues darkened, apparently at the memory. "You stopped breathing twice. I thought you were going to die before we could even bring you here. You have no idea how glad I was to see you open your eyes in the wee hours this morning. I was beginning to think you never would."

That was all very sweet, but beside the point. "The car?"

"It's still down in the canyon. The men say it's down there for good."

"For *good?*" I sat up, ignoring the clashing in my head. "My radio's down there! My phone! Not to mention how pis– angry the captain's going to be when she finds out." I took a breath. "Wait. Maybe someone found my phone. I had it in my pocket, but it's gone now. Hand me my jacket. It could be there."

"Phone? In your pocket?" The look of bafflement on her face would have been funny under other circumstances.

"You know. My cell phone. Don't you have one? Everybody should, in case of emergency. Although it's not doing me much good now, dammit." When she continued to stare at me, I added impatiently, "Sorry. If you're not going to let me get up and get dressed, could you at least let me go through my pockets?"

Silently she rose and brought me my uniform, shoes and all. I picked the trousers up with my good hand and shook them. Nothing fell out. Frustrated, I said, "Could you please hold them for me while I check them?" Frowning, she did as I asked.

With her help, I went through every single pocket in my uniform, starting with my trousers, which is where the stupid phone should have been. Everything else was there. My badge and my wallet in my trouser pockets, the pen in the pocket protector in the chest pocket of my shirt. But no cell phone. Not anywhere.

"It must have fallen out. I need to go look for it."

"You aren't in any shape to go tromping around down in that canyon," she said firmly, her hand on my chest. It was warm and a little bit rough through my t-shirt.

"I need that phone," I told her right back. "I wrecked a patrol car. I haven't reported in. They've got no clue where I am so they're going to be searching everywhere but here. How many miles off the highway is this place, anyway?"

She gave me an evasive look. "I'm not sure, exactly."

"A ballpark figure, then," I said impatiently.

"I, um, I'll go set the men to looking for your – phone."

She gave me a look I couldn't quite interpret. "If you'll tell me what it looks like."

"It's your basic iPhone. Nothing fancy."

"Eye-Phone?"

I stared at her. "Just how long *have* you been out in the back of beyond?"

She pursed her lips at me. "Just give me a description so they'll know what they're looking for."

"It's about the size of a deck of cards, with a screen. They'll know it when they see it. Trust me."

"All right." She jumped up. I'll let them know."

"Wait."

"I'll be back in a minute. I promise."

And she ran off. Again.

CHAPTER 3

She didn't know what an iPhone was? How could anyone not know what an iPhone was? I stared around the room, and the questions began to multiply.

I hadn't been paying attention. I guess I could have blamed it on the concussion, but if I'd hit my head that hard, I'd have cracked something. I should explain. This isn't the first concussion I've ever had. I played football in high school, even hoped for a college scholarship before I got my bell rung hard enough that Dad pulled me out of the program. He said a scholarship wouldn't do me any good if I didn't have any brains left to study with. Since by that time I'd about decided to go to the state police academy, anyway, I didn't argue as hard as I could have.

Anyway, I knew what a concussion felt like, and this wasn't it. I'm not sure what it was, but at least the symptoms were fading, faster than I had a right to expect them to.

I wasn't positive I believed that whole "you almost died" thing, either, because I wouldn't be recovering this fast if I had.

Which brought me right back to where I was. Plain white walls that looked like painted paneling of some kind, a wide window looking out into a huge bare-branched maple and a bright blue sky, a couple of braided rugs on the bare wooden floor. A soft bed. Heavy quilts.

Then it dawned on me what was missing. No light switches. No electric sockets. No overhead fixtures or alarm clocks or anything. Nothing but a candle on the bedside table. I remembered that candle from the first time I woke up, but it hadn't registered at the time. A power outage was one thing, but – no electricity at all? What were these people, Amish? Or, more probably, a bunch of off-the-grid militiamen like those nuts in Montana a few years ago?

But surely I'd have been told about anyone like that when I'd been assigned to Okanogan County. Then a really scary thought dawned on me. Only if anyone knew they were here. As far off the beaten path as they were, in a district this big and remote, it was more than possible even the all-knowing sergeant had no clue.

I could be a hero. Stop 'em before they set off a bomb or sent arsenic through the mail or did whatever other nasty things they had planned.

I sat up. The dizziness and disorientation were definitely passing off. I stared down at my hand. Here was another anomaly. It was wrapped up neatly in white cotton strips, with something stiff wrapped up along with it so I couldn't bend anything, but it didn't look like any sort of cast I'd ever seen. My whole lower arm ached something fierce, although I hadn't been paying it much attention, what with everything else going on. I tried to wiggle my fingers and promptly wished I hadn't. Whatever I'd done to my arm wasn't a good thing.

"Don't do that."

I glanced up. The little doctor was back, and she was scowling at me. "Why not?"

"Your wrist is broken. You need to let it rest and heal."

I let it go. It didn't take a genius to realize she was probably right. "Did you find my phone?"

She shook her head.

"Did you look for it?"

"Not personally, no. But the men have been going up and down the hillside."

"Would you give it to me if you had found it?"

She gave me a puzzled glance, then came over and took my hand. After inspecting it, she said, "It doesn't look like you've done it any damage. Please don't try to use it until I give you leave to do so."

Great. Well, it was only one hand. "Do I have a choice?"

Her lips curved slightly. She had nice lips. Smooth and pink. She's not your type, I told myself. And, besides, if my guess was right, she was a member of a crackpot bunch of anti-government militiamen who didn't believe in electricity, or anything else for that matter.

Still. Definitely not my type. "You will bring me my phone when you find it."

"If we find it, we will certainly not keep your property from you." She touched my head, presumably where I'd taken the hit in the accident. "Does that hurt?"

Her fingers were cool and dry. They tingled against my skin, but I ignored the feeling. "No."

If she felt it, she was doing a darned good job of ignoring it, too. "Good. You're a fast healer, aren't you?"

"Not particularly."

"Well, then, maybe the concussion wasn't as severe as I thought it was."

I frowned at her. "Good. Then there's no reason I can't get up and get dressed."

She frowned back at me. "I suppose not."

"Good," I said again, and swung my feet around so they hung over the edge of the bed. The world didn't sway nearly so much as it had the last time. I took a deep breath.

"Mind your hand." But she was helping me do just that, putting one hand under my elbow and the other under my wrist. "Careful, now."

"I'm fine." I wasn't, not exactly. I was still a little dizzy, but I wasn't about to admit it to her. I pushed with my good hand, and stood with my bare feet on the rag rug beside the bed.

And looked down. And down. Good grief. I'd known she was short, but – "Are you some kind of midget?"

She scowled up at me. "No, I am almost five feet tall. Are you some sort of giant?"

I wanted to laugh, she looked so pissed at me. "I'm six foot three."

"So your driver's license said, Daniel Reilly."

I quit grinning at her. "Dan, not Daniel. I thought you said you hadn't messed with my stuff."

"I did not" – a slight hesitation – "mess with it. I merely looked at it."

"Curious, were you?" I couldn't blame her.

But she looked sheepish, anyway. "Well, yes. Wouldn't you be?"

Her reaction amused me. "So, what else did you figure out while you were messing with my stuff?"

"You're a city boy," she said flatly.

"The address on my license says Omak. If you think that's a big city, you're crazy."

"Nevertheless."

I was a city boy, for all the good it was doing me now. No point in denying it any further. "Go on."

"And you're from the other side of the mountains."

"I'd almost have to be, to be a city boy."

She ignored that. "You have a girlfriend."

That surprised me, both that she'd figured it out and that it seemed to annoy her. "Had. How do you figure?"

"There was a photo. Had?"

There was? I thought I'd pitched everything I had possessed of Linda in the trash before I left Seattle. I guess I'd missed that one. "Had. She dumped me when I got stuck out here in the back of beyond. Go on." I picked up my wallet and tried to thumb it open one-handed. Amy reached over and opened it for me. Yup, there Linda was, laughing at the camera. At me. "Could you take it out and throw it away, please?"

"Of course." She eased it out of the plastic sleeve, then looked up at me. "If you're sure."

"I'm sure." Not a doubt in my mind.

But she didn't take it to a garbage can. There didn't seem to be one in the room. She looked down at it. "She's pretty."

Linda was beautiful, and she'd known it and flaunted it. I'd been proud of her looks, and so had she. I shrugged, suddenly conscious of the fact that I was standing there in my underwear. I hated to ask, but there was no way I could put my uniform back on without assistance. "Could you help me get dressed, please?"

"Oh!" She stuffed the photo in the pocket of her trousers and picked up my shirt. "Of course."

Dressed, I felt less at a disadvantage, but the process took it out of me. I was breathing hard by the time it was done. I let Amy lead me to the lone chair in the room and leaned back with my eyes closed while she went to fetch something or other. When she returned with food I realized the only thing I'd eaten since lunch yesterday? the day before? was one lousy bowl of soup. Well, not lousy, it had been delicious. But not enough to keep me fueled. No wonder I was shaky.

At least this time she'd brought me something more solid. I barely took time to thank her before scarfing down the good, solid meat and potatoes she put in front of me. Someone had realized I would be eating one-handed. The slices of roast beef, dripping with gravy, had been cut into bite-sized pieces, and the baked potato had been split and was oozing with butter. Even the broccoli, not my favorite veggie, was cut into pieces I could spear with my fork and covered with some sort of sauce that actually made it taste good.

"You guys eat like this all the time?" I asked between bites.

She smiled at me, but didn't answer, just watched me inhale the food with a look in her eyes that made me feel self-conscious. Not enough to stop eating, though, or even slow down. I was giving serious consideration to licking the plate when she moved the table away. "Would you like to go for a walk, or are you up to it yet?"

A chance to see where the hell I'd landed? "I'm up to it." I stood before she could help me, just to prove I was, and only swayed a tiny bit before I caught myself.

She frowned slightly. "Give me your arm, then."

"I don't need –"

But she already had a hand under my elbow, and I figured it wasn't worth the argument. She wasn't nearly big or strong enough to keep me from pitching onto my face, but if she wanted to think she was, I wasn't going to argue. She'd almost have done me more good if I could have used her like a cane. Or stuck her under my arm like a crutch.

I stepped forward, strangely cautious, and wondered what I would see when we went outside. A stockade and some sort of subsistence farm? Or would I be facing a row of Uzis? They couldn't be all that happy with a cop landing in their midst even if they weren't militiamen but just some sort of off-the-grid hippies, but I was pretty darned sure they wouldn't have gone to all the trouble of rescuing me only to murder me.

I don't think I've ever been so – anticipatory? – in my life. Not even when I got accepted into the patrol academy. Not even when I proposed to Linda. I'd forgotten what it felt like since my life fell apart, and I went with it. I was finally going to find out where the hell I'd landed. And what the hell I was going to do about it.

The door from my room led into a small hallway, dim but for the few streaks of light coming from a couple of open doors along the way. I glanced through them as we walked past. About as plain and spartan as my bedroom, with a few tables and chairs and rag rugs scattered about. One looked like some sort of primitive kitchen, with a pot sitting on a woodstove, a sink with – was that a pump? – and some dishes on a table nearby, but it didn't look like that was where the food had actually been cooked. I stopped.

Amy glanced up at me. "Are you still hungry?"

I could have eaten more, but I was okay for now. "No." I started forward again, and she moved with me. The door at the end of the hall beckoned like a crooked finger, gray light glowing in from outside through a small-paned leaded glass window next to it.

Amy stopped by a little table. "Wait here while I get the door." She let go of my elbow, and I grabbed at the table. I was still shakier than I wanted to admit.

She set her hand on the old-fashioned glass doorknob and hesitated. "Go on," I said. I could see her visibly steeling herself. "What are you waiting for?" For me to fall down so she could make me go back to bed and delay this even longer? I wouldn't have put it past her. But she was the one who'd suggested this walk. Why the sudden reluctance?

She took a deep breath – I could see her breasts rising under her shirt – and threw open the door with a bang that made the windowpanes rattle.

I couldn't see much at first, just a bit of dirt road and a cluster of larches on the other side of it. The house had a porch of silvery aged wood that hadn't seen a coat of paint in a long, long time. I waited, whether I wanted to or not, for Amy to come back to me and put the hand I didn't want to admit I needed back under my elbow, but she didn't make a move. I guess she was waiting for me, too.

I hoped I wouldn't fall flat on my face, and let go of the table. Took one step, then another, then finally I was at the door. I leaned on the jamb and looked out. Stared.

I was looking at a ghost town. Silver-gray buildings of weathered wood stood in various stages of tumbling down between the larch and maple trees lining the overgrown dirt road. The weeds were knee-high even right in the middle of it. Broken glass in the occasional window glinted in a stray bit of light soaking through the clouds.

I looked back inside. Reasonably fresh paint, dusted furniture, clean floors. Then I looked out again, at the silvery, tilted, creaky boards of the weathered porch.

"What the hell is going on here?" Amy winced, but I wasn't about to apologize this time. "Where the hell are we?"

"The town's name is Conconully," she replied.

I could feel my mouth drop open. "Concon– You're insane."

"It's a perfectly good name."

"That's not the point. Conconully's a ghost town." It was a famous ghost town, actually. Even I knew about Conconully, and I'd only been living in Okanogan County for two lousy months. Site of a purportedly fabulous gold strike in the 1880s, one of the richest cities in the nation and county seat for three years before a flood of 'Biblical

proportions' had wiped it off the map, these days it was nothing but –
"It's a historical marker on the side of the road. The marker said the
flood washed everything away."

"Obviously it didn't," Amy said. "I've read that marker." She put
her hand under my elbow again. "It's mostly right, but not completely.
People do still live here. Come on. Let me show you around."

Why? "Doesn't look like there's much to see."

"Oh, you'd be surprised." She tugged at my elbow, and I
thought, well, what the hell, and went with her.

Getting across that wobbly porch and down the creaking steps
was a challenge, but the rough road was easier to navigate than I'd
thought it would be. We strolled along it, the grass rustling against my
trousers, a chilly breeze batting the maple leaves around above our heads
and causing the clouds to flash sunlight off and on. Amy didn't seem to
notice the cold in her jeans and long-sleeved shirt, but I was glad of my
uniform jacket.

We passed by several heaps of lumber that must have been
buildings at some point, before Amy stopped in front of a larger one
that hadn't quite been pulled down by blackberry vines and age. The big,
dirty front window looked like someone had thrown a football through
it, and I wouldn't have stepped up on the front porch, where three
ancient rocking chairs still sat, on a bet. As I watched, though, one of
the chairs moved, almost as if someone was rocking in it. It's the breeze,
I told myself. Never mind that the other two rockers were absolutely
still. No, there went one of the others. Now I really was imagining
things.

I shook my head and forcibly brought my attention back to Amy.
"This is Madson's. It's the general store." She smiled impishly up at me.
"The selection doesn't look like much, but you'd be amazed at what you
can find in there."

I stared at her. She had to be joking, but she was already moving on. I followed, helplessly.

"That's Ballerby the druggist." Amy pointed at a square, squat building whose windows and plank walls were in even worse shape. A round sign was faded into illegibility, and the roof was half caved in. She grimaced. "Not that Mr. Ballerby carries anything of much use."

I choked. "I guess not."

She ignored me and gestured at a building two doors down, which wasn't much more than a shack, its roof collapsed at one corner. "That's the assayist's. Do you know what an assayist is?"

I didn't, but I didn't want to admit it. "Yes."

"No, you don't." But she sounded amused. "That's where the miners take their gold to have it valued."

"People are still mining around here?" If they were I bet they weren't taking their gold to that tumbledown shack.

"Well, the mines aren't what they used to be, at least according to Max." She paused, and shook her head, as if at something – or someone? – I couldn't see. I was beginning to wonder what she was seeing that I wasn't. Especially as she kept talking about this ghost town as if it were a going concern. "But then nothing is."

I thought about my current situation. "You've got that right. Who's Max?"

Again she ignored my question, and went on almost as if by rote as we strolled down through what must have been quite a town in its day, if her descriptions were to be believed, which I wasn't sure I did. "That's the First National Bank of Conconully." She sounded almost proud. "Millions of dollars in gold have passed through it, more than any other bank since Washington became a state."

Washington, as I'd learned in my high school history class, became a state in 1889. According to the historical marker the

Conconully flood had happened a mere five years later. But these buildings didn't look as if they'd been through a flood. They just looked abandoned. The bank looked like the Old West version of a ruined Greek temple, with pillars leaning drunkenly at odd angles and its elaborately heavy metal door half off its hinges. "It must have been something in its day."

Amy nodded again, and smiled, but not at me. At herself? "Oh, it still is."

I supposed it was, for a ruin.

We turned a corner and left the vestiges of Conconully's commercial district behind. This street, if I could call it that, was in slightly better repair than the main drag. The grass was crushed down as if wheels had been passing over it recently. The infamous Audrey's truck, maybe? The tracks didn't look wide enough to belong to truck tires.

I wanted to stop and take a look, but Amy tugged me along, gesturing again. "That's Belinda's shop."

This building looked to be in a bit better shape, too. At least it didn't look like it was about to fall over.

She went on, sounding now like she was talking about a friend. "She's a seamstress. A good one, too, although she's a bit old-fashioned."

I couldn't quite help the sarcasm. "Like everything else here?"

Again it was as if she hadn't heard me. "And that's Audrey's house. She's the one who's been cooking for you."

The tire tracks didn't turn in here, and I didn't see a truck or a garage or even a barn. And I was getting tired of being ignored. I stopped dead. "Audrey. Wait a minute. Isn't that who you said led me into chasing her?"

Amy cast me an annoyed glance, let go of my elbow, and kept walking.

"Wait a minute." But instead of coming back to me as I'd hoped she would – I was still shakier on my feet than I wanted to admit – she only shook her head at me and waited for me to catch up.

What choice did I have? The last thing I wanted to do was pitch face first into the weedy track, which seemed like a very real possibility as soon as she'd let go of me. So I took a step, then another, and as I caught up with her I promised myself I'd be back as soon as I could manage on my own.

We rounded another corner, back onto the main street as best as I could tell, although I'm ashamed to admit I was getting a bit turned around, which made no sense. After all, we'd only walked about the same distance as a couple of city blocks. I should have known exactly where I was.

Amy stopped in front of the largest structure I'd seen so far, two tall stories and about twice as broad as the bank, and the one in by far the best repair. Even the street in front of it was smoother. No grass grew in the packed dirt still showing ruts I was pretty sure hadn't come from the tires of any car or truck tire I'd ever seen.

The building itself had a pale blue paint job that didn't look all that old, and pillars like those at the bank held up the front corners. Smaller versions of those columns stood on either side of each of the two plate glass bay windows, their huge panes miraculously still intact. And as clear as if someone had taken a bottle of Windex to them this morning.

Amy smiled at the life-sized pig front and center in the right-hand window and let out her breath in what almost sounded like relief. The pig appeared to be molded from plaster or clay of some kind, its outer layers peeling in places, but for some reason I didn't think that was the case. And it looked – it looked positively smug. I'd never seen such a lifelike expression on an inanimate object before, let alone on a plaster pig.

I couldn't help asking, in spite of her refusal to answer my questions so far. "Who's the pig?"

To my surprise she didn't ignore me this time. "I called him Wilbur until I was corrected," she told me.

I snorted.

"What?" Her mouth quirked as she turned to watch me. "You never read *Charlotte's Web*? Or were you too busy reading the Hardy Boys and wanting to be a cop when you grew up?"

I shook my head. "I caught the reference, thanks."

"His real name is Harry."

"That's nice," I answered without thinking. "Where'd he come from? It's a weird thing to see in a store window." Although not, I thought, nearly as weird as everything else that had happened to me in the last forty-eight hours. I stopped and turned to give her my best cop glare, pulling my elbow out of her hand. I didn't need it anymore, I realized suddenly. "You're doing a helluva job of distracting me. What's going on here? Where are those people I saw yesterday? Where am I, really?"

She didn't answer any of my questions. Instead she said, "We found your phone."

"Well, thank God," I said. "Give it to me."

She reached into her pocket. "I'm afraid it's not –"

"I don't care."

"All right." She pulled her hand out of her pocket and held it out to me.

I groaned.

"I'm afraid it didn't survive your crash. I'm sorry."

That was an understatement. The screen was absolutely shattered, what was left of it, and I could see the cracked innards through a tear in the plastic film. "Was it run over?" It *looked* like someone had pounded on it with a hammer.

She shrugged. "It very well could have been."

"How? It was in my pocket–" My *trouser* pocket. No way it could have flown out of my trouser pocket, but the proof it had was in my hand. And bounced off a tree or something and under the wheels of the Vic? That must have been quite a feat. But why would someone have damaged it deliberately? Well, how it had happened was beside the point. It was surely dead now, and the way it had accomplished the trick didn't really matter.

"I'm sorry," she said again.

"Hey, it's not your fault." Even if I really needed to blame someone just now. "I didn't think to ask, since you look like you're pretty cut off from the rest of the world, but there's not a landline somewhere around here I could use, is there?"

"A landline?" That puzzled look again.

"Or a cell phone I could borrow?"

She laughed, but somehow I didn't think she was amused. "No telephones here, I'm afraid."

"I figured as much. Why? No reception down here in this godforsaken place?"

"No wires. You might have noticed the lack of power lines as well."

"I did. Why?"

She didn't answer me again, but went on with her tour. "This was the richest town in Washington a century ago. Doesn't look like it now, does it?"

"No, but– a century ago? I thought you said this place boomed in the 1880s? That's way more than a century ago."

Had that startled her? If it had, she hid it almost instantly. "Well, give or take. Those stone pillars were carved of marble brought all the way from Idaho."

I let it go. Somehow I didn't think she'd answer me even if I badgered her. It wasn't like she was answering anything else I asked, and this was hardly the first question I wanted answered. Instead I ran a hand over the pitted flutes of one of the pillars. It felt incredibly smooth, and I heard something–

"What was that?" It had sounded like a voice, way off in the distance. Like the wind, almost. But not quite.

Amy looked away. "I didn't hear anything."

How had she known I'd heard something? "You didn't hear what?"

That flustered her, at least momentarily. She glared at me. "Whatever it was you thought you heard. Come on. You've walked enough for your first try. You obviously need to get back to the house and rest."

She was right about that, blast her. And it was obvious she wasn't going to admit to having heard anything. Or anyone. I let her lead me back to, what was it? Her office? Her house? And why did it look completely abandoned on the outside and perfectly normal on the inside?

That puzzle was petty compared to all the others, though. Where was I? Really? And why was the place deserted? Where had all those people gone?

Chapter 4

I'd pretty much had it by the time Amy helped me get my boots off and I'd flopped back on that way too comfortable bed. She offered to help me get undressed again, "So you can relax," but I declined her services.

"I'm fine." I didn't intend to be down for long. She left me, and came back with more food, which I eyed skeptically for about two seconds before diving in. I had no idea where these feasts were coming from, but there was no way I was going to turn them down. I needed all the help I could get to return to normal so I could figure out how the hell to escape.

I didn't even want to think what the sergeant was assuming by now.

My wallet and smashed phone sat on the table next to the bed where I'd dropped them. I picked up my wallet. Aside from the driver's license being put back in its slot upside down, it didn't look like anyone had messed with it. I didn't know exactly how much cash I'd started Saturday with, but the small wad of bills looked untouched. Even my highway patrol badge was still in its leather holder. I let my breath out as my fingers made contact with it. It would have been the worst loss, by far.

I was just thinking how quiet the house was, when voices erupted from down the hall. I swung my legs down, shoved my feet into my boots, and, without lacing them which would have been impossible, anyway, tried to walk as quietly as possible down the hall to see what was going on.

* * *

They were in the room with the woodstove. I curled my toes into my boots so the heels wouldn't thump on the wooden floor, and crept up on the doorway. I'd already figured out if I was going to learn anything, it wouldn't be from what anyone told me directly.

Three people occupied the room. One was the little doctor, gesticulating angrily with a large wooden spoon. The second was the big, burly, gray-headed fellow who'd insisted I stay in bed yesterday. He was standing with his legs apart and his arms folded on his chest.

The one who was doing most of the talking was the tall, spindly, white-haired woman who'd stuck her head in the door earlier. She was wearing a floor-length, long-sleeved, high-collared dress and a food-splattered apron covering most of it. "The tea won't hurt him," she was saying. "I told you I chose the right one. Someone had to come. We need him."

"You had no right to make that choice for him, Audrey," Amy snapped. "Any more than you had the right to make it for me."

Audrey looked like she thought she ought to look apologetic and didn't know how. "Technically, I didn't make that choice for you."

"Technically, my foot." Amy thumped the spoon on the edge of the stove. Bits of whatever had been on it went flying in all directions. Audrey made protesting noises.

"She didn't," the big guy said in a placating tone. "You really were an accident."

Amy sighed. "I know." She set the spoon down. "But Rob, I feel like I've been an accident ever since I can remember. No purpose at all."

"You have one," Audrey told her.

"What? To keep Conconully alive? What's the point?"

"Uh-oh."

At Rob's words they all turned. "Um, hi," I said to their stares. They didn't say anything, not even a simple hi back. I forged on. "I'm thirsty. Is there anything to drink?

Audrey smirked. "Sit right down, young man. I'll pour you some tea." She gestured at the table.

I glanced at Amy. She had gone as still and white as the wall behind her. "What's wrong with the tea?" I asked.

"Whatever do you mean?" asked Audrey. She sounded like one of the kids I'd once caught trying to explain to me how he and his buddies weren't trying to break into the liquor store at one in the morning on a Saturday night.

"I'll get you some water," Rob said.

"Thanks." I sat down. "I'm not much of a tea drinker."

Amy's face sprang back to life. "I'm glad to hear that. Tea is about the only thing Audrey makes that isn't delicious, anyway, so you're not missing out."

Audrey scowled at her, but Amy went on before she had a chance to say anything. "You did say how much you liked the food I brought you. Here's a chance to compliment the cook." Her eyes were almost pleading.

I eyed Audrey, but figured there was no point in making things worse. "So you're the one who made that fantastic roast beef dinner? Thank you very much."

Audrey's face softened. "It is grand to have someone new to cook for."

I looked hopefully at her, and she laughed. Amy and Rob both did, too. "You must still be a growing boy, young man."

I looked down to my feet and back up again. "I sure hope not." The laughter this time seemed to cut the tension. It also got me fed again, starting with cold roast beef sandwiches, at a table and with company this time.

"So," I said after my second helping of apple cobbler. This sure beat the heck out of fast food or prepackaged stuff in my apartment. "I don't mean to be ungrateful, but I don't suppose one of you could give me a lift back to Omak, could you? The sergeant is going to be furious with me for not checking in, and they're probably combing the hills for me by now."

Rob looked at Audrey. Audrey looked at Amy. Amy looked out the window.

I sighed. "You didn't wreck that truck with your stunts the other night?" I asked.

"Yes, yes, I'm sorry, the truck is damaged, can't drive, won't be fixed for a while." Audrey babbled. "We'll be glad to put you up till then, no charge, no trouble."

And when she ran out of breath, Rob started in. "Can't get the parts, sorry, I don't know how long it's going to be before I can get it running again, I'm working on it."

He looked helplessly at Amy, who said flatly, "I'm not going to lie to him."

"Lie to me about what?"

"Come on." She rose.

"Amy, dear," Audrey said. She sounded genuinely worried, which was the first time she'd sounded genuine since I'd first heard her voice.

Rob added, "Kid, don't."

"Don't call me that."

"Sorry. But don't, Doc Amy, please."

Amy sighed. "I'm just going to take him back to his room. Tell the others – you'll tell the others what they want to hear, anyway. Go on." She made shooing motions at them, then gestured to me. "Come on."

From the doorway, I glanced back at Rob and Audrey. He had scootched his chair closer to hers, and had wrapped an arm around her. She leaned into him. But they were both looking at Amy. She was not looking back.

She led me down the hall to my room, and pointed to the chair. "Sit down."

She had the doctor's authoritative voice down pat. I said, "Yes, ma'am," and sat.

She smiled sadly. "Sorry. I just get fed up – never mind." She took a breath. "I don't suppose you'd want to consider staying here, would you?"

"What?!?" I jerked back to my feet.

"Sit down." She'd lost the authority in her voice. "Please."

But I couldn't sit. "Stay here? In a ghost town? Commute however many miles every day? Why?"

"I was thinking you could quit your job. That's all you've got, from what you've told me." Her smile was sympathetic, and it made me want to break something.

"That's not true, and even if it was it's beside the point."

"I suppose it is, looking at it your way." She perched herself on the side of the bed. "There. That's better. I don't have to crane my neck quite so hard."

She still had to crane it some, though. I sat down, too, the consideration basic reflex. "Is that better?"

"Yes. Thank you." She pulled one foot up and tucked it underneath her other leg. "What else would you be leaving if you stayed here?"

I hedged. "Why would I be leaving anything? This place is out in the back of beyond, sure, but it's not on another planet."

Her lips quirked. "Once you move here, it's hard to find time to get back to the real world."

I snorted. "Oh, yes, I can see how exciting it is."

"You'd be surprised." She fell silent.

After a moment, I said, "Well, like I said, it's beside the point. I've got a job, and a life, and much as I appreciate the invitation and all, I'm going to have to say no."

She jumped down and gave me a dirty look. "I wasn't implying that, you jerk."

I watched her flounce across the room as if she had Audrey's floor-length skirt at her disposal. As if she was used to having floor-length skirts at her disposal.

"Sorry," I said to her retreating back.

She whirled at the door, and if looks could kill, at the very least I'd have been flat on my back in that bed again. "I bet. Well, at least you didn't drink the damned tea."

She vanished in a huff down the hall.

"Well, I am sorry."

I sank down onto the chair again, the fingers of my left hand drumming on one arm rest, my broken right hand sitting there like a dead fish on the other. Why did they want me to stay? Audrey'd said I'd been chosen. By who? Her? And why? And how had Amy ended up here? What accident? And why couldn't she leave? She didn't seem very happy here so why was she staying?

Although I had to admit that even at her angriest she seemed to like Rob and even Audrey as much as she was frustrated with them.

But why did they want me to stay? And what the hell did a stupid cup of tea have to do with anything? I leaned back till my head was propped against the back of the chair, and closed my eyes, trying to make some sense of the whole thing and failing.

It's a ghost town, I thought drowsily. Maybe everyone's a ghost.

Yeah. And either I hit my head a lot harder than I thought I did and I'm sitting in my crashed cruiser having a heck of a hallucination, or it's still the middle of two nights ago and I'm dreaming.

"You all right?" It was Rob's voice. Odd how I hadn't heard his footsteps in the hallway. His boots were big and clunky enough he should have made all kinds of racket. He's a ghost, I reminded myself. It was the best explanation I had right now, at any rate. I lifted my head and opened my eyes. Right. First ghost I'd ever met, well, first ghost I'd ever met, period, but what kind of ghost wore flannel, jeans, and boots? Couldn't see through him, either.

"Daniel?"

"Yeah, yeah. I'm fine." Losing it, but fine.

CHAPTER 5

They left me alone for a while after that. I slept for a while, sprawled on the bed, digesting again, but when I woke I wasn't sick enough anymore to lie around all day. And, besides, why was I taking their word about my cruiser? It might not be as bad as they thought it was. Only one way to find out. I stomped into my boots again, managed to put my jacket back on, and headed out the door into the deserted street.

The problem was, I had no idea which way to go. Not that there were that many choices. Well, I had a fifty percent chance of being right, and if I was wrong, I could always turn around and come back and try the other direction.

I set out down the street.

It wasn't a bad day at all, so far as November weather went. Cool, breezy, clouds scudding across a sky much bluer than I'd been used to on the other side of the mountains. And dry, dry air. I licked my lips and tasted dust.

Conconully ghost town was bigger than I'd realized from the stroll Amy and I had taken yesterday. The larger buildings of downtown petered out pretty quickly, but there were dozens of houses.

Some of them were in pretty good condition, actually, for having been abandoned for well over a hundred years. I wondered which ones the faces at my window occupied. And if their insides were as much of a mismatch with their outsides as the building where I'd been housed.

I'd just about reached the edge of town and decided I'd chosen the wrong direction when I caught a glimpse of the woman.

It was definitely a her, and someone I hadn't met before, although what a little old lady in a long skirt was doing up in that tree was beyond me. She grinned down at me. I grinned back. "Nice view?"

"Oh, yes."

"Can you see a police car from up there?"

"What's a 'police car'?"

"You know. A car with lights on the top. The one I'm looking for says 'Washington State Patrol' on the side."

She shook her head, then slid down from her perch and ran off, a lot more agilely than I'd have expected from her looks.

"Hey!" I called. She didn't stop and she didn't turn back. After a moment she rounded the corner of a building and vanished.

"That was rude." I'd just asked her a simple question. But I'd about decided this was the wrong direction, anyway, and turned around.

I was almost back to 'my' building, when Amy caught up with me. She was out of breath and looked worried. "Where have you been?"

For some reason I was reluctant to tell her my real purpose. "I was feeling cooped up. I went for a walk."

"Oh. Well, I could use your help, if you're feeling up to it."

"My help?"

"Yes. We've been having a problem, and you're a cop, you might be able to do something about it."

That startled me. "You've got a crime kind of problem?"

"I guess." When she didn't say anything more, I stopped and looked at her. I knew that expression. She looked as if she wished she hadn't said anything.

"Well, what is it? I can't read your mind."

"Someone's been stealing things."

I raised my eyebrows.

She sighed and said, "Important things. Well, one important thing."

I looked around at the abandoned – well, it wasn't completely abandoned, was it? – town, and then back at her. "Lots of important things around here, are there?"

"Oh, never mind. I should have known you'd say something like that. Even if you are a police officer." She started off down the street again.

I caught up to her. "Highway patrol. I don't usually handle theft. But I've had the training. I'll be glad to help."

She stopped again. "You have to promise not to laugh."

Okay, this was getting weirder and weirder. "I promise."

"Someone stole Harry."

Harry? Wait a minute. "Someone stole that old pig?"

"Yes." She looked like she was about to cry. "And while he's just a battered old plaster pig to you, he matters to some of us–" She stopped, tried to catch her breath. I had her by the arm now. "He matters to me."

"Okay. I'm not laughing."

She sniffed. "Thank you."

I headed toward the big building on the side street where he'd resided in the display window the day before. "When did you last see him?"

"Just now, on my way home after checking on you. When—"
she gulped like she was swallowing tears "— I looked in the window, just
like I always do, and he was gone."

"You sure someone's not just playing a trick on you? Teenagers
on a dare or something like that?" The pig could be clear back in
Omak by now, sitting in the high school principal's office or some
damned thing.

"That building is locked," she said firmly.

We'd arrived at the storefront. "Amy?"

"Yes?"

"I hate to tell you this, but I could break into any building here
in less than five minutes."

"Oh, just look, will you?" she said, the disgust plain in her
voice. She pointed.

I looked. The display window looked exactly as it had when I'd
seen it yesterday. Not a dust mote out of place. Except for one rather
large exception. Harry the pig was gone, all right.

I looked back at Amy. "Okay, what's going on here?"

She still looked just as stricken, but there was something in her
eyes. "Harry's gone. Can't you see?"

"Yes. But that's not the only thing going on here. The dust has
to be inches thick in there, but there aren't any footprints."

"It is not dusty in there," she said indignantly.

"You are not going to tell me you clean inside every building in
this town."

"I don't, of course."

"Neither does Audrey. Neither does Rob."

"Well, of course not."

"Unlock the door, Amy."

"Why? You can see he's gone."

"I can't help you if I can't investigate the scene of the crime."

Her face fell. "Oh."

"Yeah." I turned away. "Anyway, I've got more important things to do than investigate the theft of a plaster pig."

She stood where I left her as I strode off, but her plaintive voice carried on the wind. "Like what?"

I called back. "Like find my cruiser."

"Oh."

I must have walked miles that afternoon. I went up one direction and down the other, but never even saw anything resembling the canyon they'd told me the cruiser had crashed down into. The landscape was almost uniformly rolling and gentle alongside the road, no matter where I looked.

The trees lining the track were unmarked by anything looking like a vehicle crash. The road's surface, such as it was, didn't show a single skid mark, either.

The sun was almost gone behind the trees when I finally gave up and headed back into town. My feet were sore from walking in my unlaced boots and my head was aching and my stomach was growling. Again. It was as if I hadn't eaten in days.

And when I finally made it back, the place just reached out at me. The setting sun glinted in the broken windows, looking almost like lamplight. There was a light in the one building, or, to be more accurate, on the porch. Someone stood with one hand on the railing next to a lamp, peering into the dusk. It had to be Amy, given her height, but that was about all I could tell.

"There you are." Yes, it was Amy, and she sounded inordinately pleased to see me. No mention of my having taken off. Or of my refusal to do anything about her stupid pig.

"Yeah. Here I am."

"Are you hungry? Audrey roasted a chicken and made dressing. She makes terrific dressing."

My stomach growled again. What the hell. I was starving, and I could quiz her again over dinner. Or I could try, anyway.

I shrugged. "Sure. That sounds great."

CHAPTER 6

"So," she said brightly as she led me into the kitchen, where that roast chicken was sending up an odor that made my mouth water. The table was neatly set for two, with fancy silverware and even a pair of wine glasses. "Did you enjoy your walk?"

"Aren't Audrey and Rob eating with us?"

She shook her head. "They've gone home for the evening."

I pulled out a chair for her, since she seemed to be expecting me to, and seated myself. Then I took my first good look at her. "What's the occasion?"

"I got tired of jeans. I do, occasionally."

The long pale blue dress was pretty, in a dainty froofy sort of way. It didn't suit her, somehow.

"Do you like wine?"

I shrugged. "I'm more of a beer kind of guy, but I'll try some if you are."

She smiled, uncorked the wine, and poured.

She raised her glass to me. I shook my head. "You want to make a toast or something?"

"It is traditional."

I raised mine and clinked it to hers. "Where is my cruiser, Amy?"

"That's not a toast," she said, sounding almost confused.

"No, but it's what I need to know."

"I don't know exactly."

"Amy, I didn't see anything remotely resembling a canyon for a long way in either direction heading out of this town."

"Well, if it's where I think it is, it's farther out than that."

"In which direction?"

She tried to hand me the knife. "Would you carve the chicken please? I always make a mess of it."

"How am I supposed to do that with a broken wrist?"

She just stared at me for a second, then said, "The chicken's getting cold."

I stared down at my hand and realized that somewhere, somehow, along the way, the bandages had fallen off. I flexed my wrist, then my fingers, and picked up the knife. And it felt just fine. I shook my head, trying not to freak out, and stuck to my guns. "Would you answer my question, please?"

"I don't know."

"You don't know what? Whether you'll tell me or not? Let me tell you something. If you don't tell me—"

"I don't know which direction."

"*What?*"

"Would you *please* quit brandishing that knife and carve the blessed chicken?"

I couldn't help it. In spite of everything, I laughed. "I doubt that chicken ever thought it was blessed."

Her shoulders slumped. "Just do it. Please."

Instead I set the carving knife down. "What's going on here? Really?"

She sounded almost desperate. "Dan, can't you trust me? Please?"

"Trust you to what? Get me out of here? I don't know why, but you seem to want to keep me here whether I want to stay or not. Why should I trust you?"

She sighed, and picked up the knife. "It'll be your fault if you end up eating mangled chicken."

"It's all mangled by the time it hits our stomachs, anyway."

She glanced up from her work on the bird. "That's true." She took a deep breath. "There are things I can't tell you without getting permission. And I can't get permission yet. I'm sorry. I'm working on it."

I didn't know what to say to that. None of it made any sense. Why should she need permission – and from who? – to answer my questions? Why would they want to hold a cop captive? I'd about given up on the idea of this place being some sort of anti-government militia compound, like the Weavers over in Idaho or those nuts down in Waco, Texas. Besides, that sort of thing had gone out of style after 9/11. And nobody here'd been brandishing guns at me.

Guns. Oh, shit. I couldn't believe I'd spaced *that* out. I really must have had a concussion. The last I'd seen of my gun it was sitting on the seat of my cruiser. "Did your people find my gun?"

Amy looked startled, but swallowed and answered me. "Yes. It's in the drawer of the table next to your bed."

The relief was overwhelming. "What? You're kidding."

"I've been surprised you haven't asked about it before now, honestly."

So was I, to put it mildly. "Why didn't you tell me it was there?"

"I was asked not to."

"By who?" I stood and pushed back my chair.

She set down the knife. "It's not like we hid it from you. Where are you going?"

"To see if you're telling me the truth."

She got up and followed me into the bedroom. I yanked open the drawer. At least it wasn't in quite as bad a shape as the phone. It was only broken into three pieces. Three battered pieces I wasn't going to be able to put back together. I'm not sure anyone was going to be able to put those pieces back together. And it didn't look like car wreck damage. It looked deliberate. Just like the phone. *Why?*

She had that pleading expression on her face again. "I-I'm sorry." She did look like she meant it.

I wondered how many other troopers had both wrecked their cruiser and had their gun trashed in their first two months of service, and winced. "I swear everything I owned that mattered was destroyed in that wreck."

"Well, not quite." She sounded quite sure of herself for someone who couldn't possibly have a clue.

I practically shot the words at her. "Tell me what wasn't. The cruiser, my phone, my gun..."

"You're still here."

That brought me to a halt. "Yeah." I owed her an apology for that one. "That's a helluva way to thank you for saving my life."

"It's all right." Her lips quirked.

"Maybe to you."

She took my arm. "Come on. Supper's getting cold."

When we were back at the table, she said, "You don't seem all that happy about having had your life saved. Were things really so bad for you?"

That was an odd way to look at it. "I'm sorry if I haven't seemed very grateful up till now. It's just – I can't help but think about what's going on out there. They've got to be going crazy by now, looking for me. I should have radioed in about chasing your friend Audrey, but I didn't, so they have no idea where I am. From their point of view, I just vanished off the face of the earth."

"So people are worrying about you? Anyone in particular?"

"I suppose they've notified my dad by now. Maybe he even dragged himself away from his law practice to come badger the searchers. I doubt Carol could get away, though, even if she wanted to. Somebody'd have to stay and watch the kids."

"You have brothers and sisters?"

"Two half-brothers and a half-sister." Who I barely knew. They were more like nieces and nephews, age wise, and Dad and Carol hadn't exactly pushed us to stay in touch after I left home. To be honest, I hadn't made much of an effort, either.

"That sounds nice."

"I guess."

"Anyone else?"

I grimaced. "You know about the girlfriend situation. I'm more worried about everybody back at the station. Search and rescue is expensive, and I barely got hired on as it was."

"So you're unhappy about being a burden."

If she wanted to look at it that way. "Yeah. I've only been on the job two months. I really wanted to show the taxpayers they hadn't made a mistake hiring me in this economy. And here I am already costing them more money than I'm worth."

She gave me an odd look. "How much *are* you worth, Dan?"

I shrugged. "Sorry. I didn't mean to go off on that riff. You're just too easy to talk to." It was true, dammit. She smiled as if I'd given her a compliment. I cast about for a brighter subject. "So. Now I've proved I can't even find my own cruiser–" Oops.

Brighter, dammit. "Sorry, sorry." I was a damned sorry son of a bitch. "Anyway, since I've got some time on my hands before I can get out of here, apparently, the least I can do is try to help you find Harry the pig."

"That's all right." She took a sip of wine as we finished our chicken and dressing. "Would you like some cherry pie?"

"I swear, if I keep eating like this they're going to have to roll me out of here when they do find me."

"Oh, you don't look like a few extra pounds will go amiss."

I looked at her slim body. "Do you guys eat like this all the time, or is this just for me?"

She smiled, but there was something in her eyes. "Audrey enjoys a new audience for her talent."

"So she said." I wanted to see Amy smile without that something in her eyes, but I had no idea if it was me putting that hint of sadness in them or if it was something else altogether. It couldn't be that stupid pig. "Sure. Bring it on."

The pie, like everything else I'd put in my mouth since I'd awakened in this bizarre place, was incredible. Juicy, tart, the crust flaky enough to melt in my mouth. "God. Audrey could be making a fortune in some fancy restaurant in Seattle. What's she doing out here?"

Amy looked startled. "You should tell her that."

"Maybe I will."

"But she likes it here."

"She must." I swallowed the last bite and heroically did not ask for seconds. "So. Tell me everything you know about Harry."

She rose and started to clear the table. "It's not that big a deal."

"Yeah, it is. Sit down and tell me about it." I pointed to the chair.

She sat back down. "He was a gift. When I first arrived here. They said he'd been found near where they found me, so he must be mine. But I don't remember him from before here."

"You're not from here, either?"

She put her hand over her mouth.

"Look, like you said, it's not that big a deal. I'd figured you weren't. What I want to know is why you stayed."

Her hand went back to her lap. "I thought you wanted to know about Harry."

I sighed, deflected again. "Sure. So if he's yours, why was he in that storefront window?"

She looked down at her empty saucer. "This is going to sound silly."

"Trust me," I told her dryly. "It can't get much sillier than it already is."

To my pleased astonishment, she giggled. Now normally I'm not much for that kind of thing, but hers, well, it was different. It lightened her face, and her entire demeanor, and it exposed a dimple in her cheek I'd never have known was there before. She should have looked like Shirley Temple sitting there in that dress giggling with her hair all curled and her big blue eyes and that dimple, but she didn't. She looked like Amy. And that was a very fine way to look.

"This really isn't fair," I told her.

"What's not fair?"

"You know, Doc Amy, you know so much about me, you've been through my wallet and asked me practically everything, but I don't even know your last name."

She held out her hand. "Amy Melissa Duvall."

I reached across the table and shook it. "Nice to meet you. Daniel Benjamin Reilly."

She giggled again. "I'm not a doctor, by the way. Just an EMT. Emergency–"

"Medical Technician," I finished with her and added, "There's no 'just' about being an EMT."

She positively beamed at me. "They don't really understand the distinction here. It's nice to meet someone who does."

We were really getting sidetracked. I tucked that line away for further inquiry later and tried to get back to the subject. Which was? Oh.

"So, Ms. Duvall. What's so silly about Harry the pig residing in the storefront window?"

She sobered. I almost regretted bringing her back to the point. "He's become sort of the town mascot. They thought he was mine, because, well, because of where and when he was found, but I was pretty upset at the time, and he reminded me, well–" She took a breath.

"It's just a plaster pig," I said.

"I know. Anyway, when I decided to stay here, everybody was so happy–"

Another tidbit to ask about later.

"I asked Max if I could put it in his window and he said yes."

"So it's sort of a symbol."

She looked inordinately grateful that I'd got it. I wasn't sure I had, actually, but I wasn't about to say so.

I had to ask, though. "What made you decide to stay here?"

"The first time he disappeared–" She bit her lip.

"The first time?" But she wasn't meeting my gaze. "Is that getting too close what you don't have permission to talk about?"

She nodded.

"Whose permission?"

She started stacking dishes. I put my hand on her arm. "Look, I'll help you find Harry. But when we do get him back where he belongs, you're going to need to talk to whoever it is you need to get permission from to tell me what the heck's going on here, because I deserve to know."

She smiled down at me, but that sad hint was back in her eyes. "When we find him, I'll have permission."

She stood, plates in her hands. I let my hand slip off her arm. My palm felt cold without her warm skin under it.

"So," she said brightly as she headed toward the old-fashioned sink. I gathered the rest of the dishes and followed. "What would you like to do this evening? We can't go pig-hunting in the dark."

CHAPTER 7

Turns out there weren't a whole lot of options for entertainment in Conconully that night. It shocked me, I'll tell you. We ended up playing poker for a couple of hours, and taking turns cleaning each other out of a box of matchsticks. Amy couldn't bluff to save her life. But she had a way of taking full advantage of every card crossing her hand that made her win more often than she should have. She didn't see through my bluffs, though, so it evened things out.

At last she said, "I should be getting home."

"Sure you should. You're ahead, after all."

She stirred her pile of matches with a finger. "You cheat, or I'd have them all."

"Bluffing, not cheating."

She gave me a chiding look. "That's not the way I was taught."

"Then whoever taught you didn't know what they were doing."

"Probably not. But it is late." She scooped her matches up and dumped them back in the box, then started gathering up the scattered cards. I followed suit, then stopped to examine one of the cards. It was an odd-looking deck. The backs were ordinary enough, if kind of plain, but the fronts didn't have numbers, just so many hearts or spades or clubs or diamonds on each. The face cards weren't standard, either. I'd gotten used to them quickly enough, but I'd certainly never seen anything like them before.

Amy caught me examining it, and held out her hand. "Strange-looking cards," I said, handing it to her.

"Yes. They're antiques. It didn't become traditional to put actual numbers on them until later."

Later than what? But she was busy, gathering things up and putting them away.

Her coat was hanging on a rack in the hallway. Feeling like she expected me to, I held it for her as she slipped her arms into it. It wasn't much to look at, a beat-up shearling jacket that didn't go with her dress at all, but she wrapped it around herself and snuggled into it.

She glanced up at me. "It's been a very pleasant night. Thank you for the company."

"You're the one– Can I walk you home?"

She seemed to think about it so long I thought maybe I should give her an out. But I wanted to walk her home, and not just because I wanted to see where she lived. But at last she said, "Yes, I'd like that."

I put my uniform jacket back on, wishing I had something warmer, and we walked out into the sparkling night.

I'd never seen stars like that before. Growing up on the west side of the mountains, where the clouds block them nine months out of the year and the light pollution does them in the rest of the time, I never had the chance. These were so thick and bright they almost looked like they were caught in the treetops. I wanted to reach out and grab a cluster and hold them in my hand. And maybe give a few to Amy, since she was too short to stretch that high.

I looked down at her, almost embarrassed at the whimsy even if I hadn't said it aloud. She was watching me intently.

"What?"

"Nothing." She pulled her hand out of her pocket, and tucked it into the crook of my arm.

I didn't say anything, but the gesture distracted me enough I didn't realize what else I was seeing for a few seconds as we strolled down the street. Then I was flabbergasted enough to where I simply couldn't make it register.

The buildings *looked* the same, false front stores and clapboard houses and the pillared bank. But they weren't the same. Lamplight shone through whole glass windows, doors were firmly closed instead of swinging on broken hinges. Roofs were straight, not swaybacked and full of holes.

The wood was still silver in the starlight, and the grass still grew tall around the foundations, and the road was still a rutted track, but –

I stopped and stared, but I couldn't get my voice to work. Just as well, since my ears were straining for sounds that reminded me of a dog whistle, only not so high-pitched. I knew there were sounds. I just couldn't quite – hear them. Voices. Laughter. The tune of a piano, even. Was that a baby's cry?

I stared around me, realized I was holding my breath and let it out in a whoosh. Immediately the almost-sounds stopped. The lamplight went out. I didn't see it happen, but the buildings that were straight and strong one second were sagging and hollow the next. Just as they had been. A door creaked as it swayed slightly.

I found my voice. "What the *hell* happened just now?"

Amy gazed up at me inquisitively, but her grip on my arm was tight enough to cut off the blood to my hand.

"And *don't* try to pretend nothing did."

She sighed. "No, I won't." But she didn't say anything else.

After a moment I added, in sheer frustration, "Okay, who do you need to get" – I searched for an acceptable swearword and couldn't come up with one – "permission from? Because I don't care if we wake them out of a sound sleep, you're going to get it *now.*"

Amy tried to let go of my arm, but I held onto her. "I wish that were possible."

"Why isn't it?"

She tried to get loose again, but I wasn't going to let her. Not till I had at least some answers.

"That's not something either of us has any control over."

"Why not?"

She sighed again. "Dan, please let me go. This wasn't a good idea." I thought I heard her add something about "too soon," but her voice had dropped close to the level of those voices I'd almost heard. "Go on back. I'll see you in the morning."

I stayed right where I was. "No."

She looked up at me again, and the hurt and sadness in her eyes almost knocked me over. "Please?"

"Fine. Whatever." I practically tossed her hand from me and watched her walk away, her arms hugging that ragged shearling coat to her like it was her last friend. She stumbled slightly on a rut in the road, but straightened and turned a corner, vanishing behind the general store. I made a mental note about where she'd gone, thought about following her anyway, then decided it probably wouldn't get me anywhere. No point in making things worse than they were already. I liked her, in spite of everything, and she was already pretty upset. At me? Somehow I didn't think so. But if not at me, then at what?

I turned back and tromped through the starlight, which had lost its allure, past the tumbledown buildings with their broken windows and sagging roofs, to the little house that looked like all the others on the outside, but was so clean and homey on the inside.

I went to my room and undressed.

One last thought hit me as I climbed into bed. I still didn't know if the rest of the buildings looked like mine on the inside.

* * *

I awoke to a bright, sunny morning. How many days had I been here now? I tried to count, but between the fact that I wasn't sure I believed Amy about how long I'd been out after the wreck before I'd awakened in this bizarre place, and how much the concussion had messed up my thinking after I had waked up, I couldn't be sure. I wondered sardonically as I got dressed in the uniform I was getting thoroughly sick of if she'd have to get permission to tell me the truth about that, too.

But when I went into the kitchen, it was to find a completely new person waiting for me along with my breakfast. "Hello," she said as I stopped in the doorway.

"Hi. Where's Amy?"

"She's not feeling well this morning." This new person, who was short and round and rather grandmotherly-looking, smiled at me, but I swear there was just a bit of accusation in her eyes.

I hadn't done anything, but– "I'm sorry. Is there anything I can do?"

"No, no, I'm sure she'll be fine soon." She reached for a plate sitting on the back of the stove. "Breakfast is ready."

"Thank you." I sat down, and she put the plate in front of me. It was the usual delicious-looking meal, eggs and bacon and biscuits, but suddenly for the first time since I'd arrived I wasn't all that hungry.

My new companion set a pot of jam down on the table with a thump, and went to get the coffeepot. When she came back, she asked, "Why aren't you eating?"

Instead of answering, I asked my own question. "What's the matter with Amy?"

She didn't answer, either, but poured the coffee and doctored her own with cream and sugar. She looked old-fashioned, somehow, even more than the other people I'd seen here so far. Her skirts were the standard floor-length I'd seen on Audrey and the woman up the tree, but they were fuller, and her ruffled blouse had a black ribbon at the throat. Her gray-streaked hair was done up in a bun at the nape of her neck. Her gray eyes peered through a rather battered-looking pair of wire-rim glasses.

After a moment she glanced back up at me. "Are you going to waste that food?"

"Sorry." I began to eat, even though I didn't want it. It tasted like sawdust at first, but got better as I went along and realized I was hungry, almost in spite of myself. The woman's expression softened as she watched me, and when I cleaned my plate, she almost smiled.

"I'm Belinda."

"Dan. Nice to meet you."

Apparently my manners left something to be desired, because she scowled again and cleared the table. A few moments later she left altogether, without saying anything else.

I stood in the middle of the kitchen, alone.

I took a deep breath. "You said you wanted to go see if the other buildings were like this one, Reilly. Now's your golden opportunity."

* * *

The sun hurt my eyes as I stepped out onto the porch and into it. I wondered if I'd ever get used to bright sun in the wintertime, with its angle so low in the sky it was like an almost perpetual sunset. One of the porch boards snapped under my foot as I walked across it, but I jumped away and managed to keep from falling through. I was sort of relieved to get onto solid ground, though.

I stopped in the middle of the road, looking up and down at the array of buildings before me, trying to decide which one to invade first.

The houses were out of the running, at least to start. It felt too much like invading privacy, even if they all looked like they'd been abandoned for decades. For a hundred and thirty years, if the historical society sign about the great flood here was to be believed. It was amazing they were still standing, actually.

I decided to start with the building Harry had gone missing from. I could kill two birds with one stone, satisfy my curiosity and see what clues I could find to solve the theft at the same time.

I started down the street, glad to feel like I had some sort of purpose – for now, anyway. But before I'd walked more than a few yards, a boy came running at me from around the bank building.

"Mister! Hey, Mister!"

CHAPTER 8

I stopped, startled. The kid was by far the youngest person I'd seen since I got here. He was probably about my half-brother Con's age, nine or ten, short and chubby and freckled, with the kind of brown hair that looks silver in some lights. Like everyone I'd seen here but Amy, of course, he was oddly-dressed, in a dirty white shirt with full sleeves, suspenders, and knee-length trousers, with a cap stuck on his head. I was getting used to it. Everyone here dressed like they lived in a historical movie, so I didn't even pay much attention to it anymore.

It wasn't what was important, anyway. He grabbed me by the hand and started dragging me along. "You've gotta help."

"Help with what?"

"Betsy. She fell down the well."

I almost laughed. Now what had I wandered into, an old episode of *Lassie*?

But the kid must have caught my expression, because suddenly I'd managed to piss off yet another of the strange residents of this strange place. "It's not funny, Mister."

I sobered my expression. "I'm sorry. You're right. What do you want me to do?"

"You're the sheriff, aren't you?" He gave me a pleading look, but he didn't slow down.

Sheriff??? Where the hell had the kid gotten that idea? Not from Amy. I was as sure of that as I could be of anything. "Pulling people out of wells is part of the sheriff's job description here?"

The kid just gave me another 'what's your problem' look and kept going. We passed the bank and turned down a side track, past a couple of houses and over a rise. I could hear people. Lots of people. And not just out of the range of my hearing, either, but real voices.

"Albert, you idiot, that's not going to reach."

"You got a better idea?"

"Give me that."

"Why?"

And a wail that sounded like it was coming from the bottom of a well, all right.

The problem was, there wasn't anybody there. Not a soul. The kid coughed. Silence dropped like a stage curtain.

Oh, god. Not again. I closed my eyes for a long moment, then opened them again. The kid was still there, watching me like he wasn't sure if I'd disappear or not. But we weren't alone anymore.

Rob strode up to me. "Glad you're here. Maybe you can help. Nobody else seems to be able to." He gestured toward where the voices had been coming from. "Come on."

I stayed right where I was. I felt like I'd been planted there.

"Please, Mister?" the boy added. "That's my sister down there."

Well, that kicked in whatever I'd needed it to. "Sure, kid. Is there any rope?"

"I've got some," Rob said. "But she's only three years old. Someone's going to have to go down and bring her out."

"Three years–" I took a breath. "Why wasn't somebody watching her?"

The kid's face fell. I took in his suddenly hangdog look. "So this is your fault? Well, it's not the end of the world. I'll get her out."

His face – he had one of the most expressive faces I've ever seen – lit right back up. "Thank you, Mister."

"But you've got to promise to keep a better eye on her from now on," I told him.

The kid nodded so vigorously his cap fell off. He picked it up, dusted it off, and clapped it back on his head.

Rob told him, "You go on and get your mother, Tim."

And down again. It was like watching a yo-yo. Or a really bad actor. "Do I have to?"

"Yes. This is as much her fault as it is yours."

The kid appeared to digest this and his face lightened again. He ran off.

Rob and I hurried up to the well, which was not what I'd think of when I think of a well. It was a simple, square, wooden platform about four feet across and three inches off the ground, with a round hole about two feet in diameter cut in the middle of it. A lid obviously meant to cover the hole and keep accidents like this one from happening was leaning haphazardly off the side of the platform.

"How'd she get that cover off in the first place?" I asked Rob as he returned – when had he gone? – with a coil of rope over his shoulder.

"She didn't. Tim was fetching water for his mother." With what? I wondered. There was no sign of a bucket anywhere, although I supposed it could be at the house.

Rob handed me the rope. I tested it. Like everything else here, it looked ancient, but the fibers seemed sound.

I peered down into the hole. A small, wet, grimy face peered back up at me, and the hollow wail started up again. "It's all right," I told her. "I'm coming down to get you."

The wail ended with a gasp. Rob joined me at the hole. "Betsy, be still. The sheriff will get you out."

Him, too? I raised my eyebrows at Rob as he glanced back at me, humor in his eyes, but I could quiz him later. I tied one end of the rope to a nearby tree, tested the knot, strung the rope along to the well, and dropped it in. It looked long enough. I hoped it would be.

"You hang onto the rope, too. That tree looks sturdy, but I want a backup."

Rob nodded and got a good grip where the rope left the platform. I grabbed on, too, and carefully lowered myself through that narrow hole into the sudden dark damp.

The well was round. The sides were lined with rough stone covered in something slimy and wet. I was grateful for the lug soles of my boots giving me traction as I went down hand over hand on the thick cotton rope. Ten feet. Twenty feet. Thirty feet. I was beginning to wonder if I would run out of rope before I ran out of well.

But then my feet splashed through the water and into surprisingly soft mud at the bottom. It was about ankle deep, but not as cold as I thought it would be, either. Before I could get my bearings, a small body swarmed up my body and strangled both arms around my neck.

"Hey," I said, and got a good grip on her.

She didn't weigh much at all. I couldn't tell what she looked like down there in the dark, but the way she clung to me was all I needed to know.

I tilted her back so I could see her face as well as I could in the gloom. "Let's get you out of here, okay?"

The grubby little head nodded and went back down against my neck.

"Will you trust me?"

Another nod.

"You think can you scramble around to my back and hang on?"

The tiny arms tightened, then she climbed right over my shoulder like a monkey, her arms still around my neck. I could feel her shivering, and the wet hem of her dress slapped up against my back.

I managed, in a choked voice, "Not so hard, okay?" and shifted her grip to my shoulders. I began fashioning the dangling end of the rope into a seat sling like they'd taught us during the search and rescue module at the patrol academy.

The child's eyes grew even wider as I shifted her around again and settled her in it. There. That was the best I could do. I leaned back and yelled toward the tiny circle of light far above. "Okay, Rob! Haul her up! Slowly, please."

I turned back to the little girl. "Okay, Betsy, here goes. If you get too close to the walls on your way up, you push at 'em with your feet. But not too hard. Otherwise, just sit still. You'll be out of here in no time."

The little girl just continued to stare at me, her eyes like saucers in her dirty face. I hoped she understood the directions I'd given her, but, as I watched her slowly disappear up the long shaft, I saw one small, dirty, wet shoe reach out and push very gently, and I grinned.

Her body gradually blocked what little light made it down this far, then occluded it altogether. I heard a scream, was pretty sure it sounded happy, and waited for the rope to drop back to me.

When it did, I went up the way I'd come down. My boots gripped the slippery walls like their soles had been covered in velcro. My hands gripped the rope one after the other as the light at the top of the well got larger and larger, until at last I reached the top. What seemed like a dozen hands grasped me and pulled me out to stand, blinking like an owl, in the bright sunshine.

A cheer went up around me. A woman, about my age and in one of those old-fashioned long skirts and whose hair was the same silvery brown as her son's, flung her arms around me and wept onto the filthy shoulder of my freshly-torn uniform shirt. Her daughter, her hand in the tight grip of her brother's, watched, her other thumb in her mouth.

I patted the woman's shoulder helplessly, and looked around me as my eyes adjusted back to full daylight.

It was by far the biggest crowd I'd seen since I'd arrived in this place. At least a dozen people, in an assortment of antique outfits, of various ages and both sexes. I recognized Audrey, who was beaming at me, and Rob, who looked satisfied, and Belinda, who nodded approval. Even the tiny little old lady I'd seen in the tree was there, grinning up at me. The others were new, but familiar in the way the town was beginning to feel familiar.

The only person missing was Amy. Odd. I'd have thought this sort of thing would be her bread and butter.

The woman who was obviously Betsy's mother finally let go of me and stood back, wiping her eyes with the back of her hand. "Thank you, Sheriff. I don't know what we would have done without you."

I caught myself just before I scraped my boot through the dirt and went into an "aw, shucks" routine. "I was glad to help, ma'am."

Her smile went a bit less wobbly. The little girl, Betsy, finally managed to wiggle her hand out of her brother's and ran up to us.

"T'ank you."

I smiled down at her. "You're welcome." I knelt to look her in the eye. "Will you promise me something?"

She nodded, her face gone solemn.

"Don't you ever go near that well again. Not till you're a big, big girl."

"As big as Tim?"

I glanced up at the boy and nodded, then turned back to Betsy. "At least as big as Tim."

She nodded, still solemn. "I p'omise."

"Good. I'm going to hold you to that." I stood back up, and tried to dust myself off.

Audrey said, "Come with me, Sheriff."

CHAPTER 9

I raised my eyebrows at her peremptory tone. Audrey ignored me and gestured. The crowd broke up as I followed her back to what I was beginning to think of as my house.

"Where's Amy?" I asked as we walked.

"She's gone to the Fogle house to look after Betsy."

"Oh. Good. I wondered why she wasn't at the well along with everybody else."

Audrey didn't answer that, but led the way up the steps onto the rickety porch. I followed her, stepping gingerly. "Does anyone have a spare hammer and some nails?"

She'd already opened the door. "Why?"

I pointed at the hole from earlier. "I'd like to fix that."

She smiled. "Don't worry about it."

"I don't want to break anything else, thanks. I almost fell through it this morning."

"Then you'd better watch your step, hadn't you? Come on."

I shrugged and followed her, glad when I'd made it inside. I'd ask Rob later. I was willing to bet he knew where the tools were.

"Belinda was right," Audrey was saying. "She caught up to me this morning and asked me straight out why we hadn't sent her to you for some new clothes. I confess it simply skipped my mind."

"New clothes?"

"I'm sure you're proud of your uniform, young man, but it is in sad repair."

I looked down at myself, at the patches of mud and green algae, at the tear where I'd caught my shirt on an out flung rock on my way down the well. At my scuffed, dirty, slimy boots. "Especially after this morning."

"Why don't you take a look at those?" She pointed.

Across the bed was laid a whole set of clothes.

"Wow," I said. "Thank you. You didn't need to do that."

I stepped forward to take a better look, but before I could, Audrey chuckled. "Oh, I think we did." She cocked her head as a metallic thump rattled the floor somewhere in the house. "And there's the other thing you need."

She opened the door and gestured me down the hall into the kitchen. A round galvanized tub, just about big enough for a person to cram himself into, took up the space between the table and the stove. A stranger worked the pump, and when his bucket was full, dumped it into the tub. I shivered, knowing exactly how cold that water was, and hoped like hell they weren't expecting –

As I stared, a huge kettle on the stove began to whistle. Rob, who was standing by the stove, picked it up and added its contents to the tub. Steam rose, and I let my breath out. Audrey went to a cupboard and turned back to me with her hands full.

"Here's soap." She handed me a bar that looked like a badly-cut brownie, only green, "and a scrub-cloth and towels."

"Wow," I said again. "Thanks." A bath in the middle of the kitchen. Better than the outhouse out back, at any rate.

She smiled at me again. "It was the least we could do after what you did just now. Come on, Rob. Quit gawking, Jim, and come along. Let him get washed before the water gets cold."

They all left, Rob closing the door behind them.

She had a point. I shucked my uniform in record time, and climbed into the tub. It *was* a tight fit, but I swear a bath had never felt so good. The heat soaked through my skin and right down to every bone and muscle I possessed. The soap was a bit raw, but I was so glad to be getting *eau de well*, not to mention three? or was it four? days worth of grime off me I didn't care. I even used it to wash my hair, since there wasn't any shampoo.

I sat in that tub until the water cooled and my fingers and toes turned pruny, then I reluctantly climbed out and dried myself off with the rough cotton towel, standing on the rug in lieu of a bath mat.

I went back in the bedroom and got my first close look at the clothing on the bed. I guess I should have expected it, but it was still something of a shock. I was going to look like what's-his-name who buddied with Jackie Chan in *Shanghai Noon*.

At least jeans were fairly universal, and if these weren't Levis, they were a good imitation. But the black shirt fastened up the front with pearly buttons, and the belt looked hand-tooled. There was even a bright red bandanna, which made me want to laugh. I didn't laugh at the heavy wool coat, though. It looked a heck of a lot warmer than my uniform jacket. The underwear was, well, I've always been a briefs guy, but at least the boxers were clean, if not like any I'd ever seen before. The socks looked hand-knitted, and the boots–

I sat down on the edge of the bed and examined them. I've never owned a pair of cowboy boots. They're not exactly popular on the other side of the mountains. But I'd seen a few pairs around and about since I'd come to the Okanogan country. These looked handmade. And expensive. And uncomfortable as hell. Well, I'd only have to wear them until I cleaned my own boots back up.

I got dressed. Belinda had obviously figured out my sizes, because everything fit, which kind of astonished me. Even the boots, which were a lot more comfortable than they looked. I stomped around in them a bit to get used to them, then gathered up my filthy uniform and went out to the kitchen.

"Well, don't you look handsome," Audrey said. She rose to take the dirty bundle from me.

I could feel the blood rushing to my face, and tried to keep hold of the uniform, but she wrested it from me before I could stop her. "Thank you. I think."

She set the clothes down on a stool, eyeing me as if to say, "don't you touch those," and went to the stove. "Would you like a cup of tea?"

"No, no thanks. How's Betsy? Have you heard?"

"Doc Amy says she's just fine. A little scraped up, but she was very lucky. No bumps on the head or anywhere else it matters."

Well, that was a relief, although given what I'd seen of her after I got her out I wasn't surprised. "I'm glad to hear it. I'd like to go see for myself, though." I was less concerned about little Betsy than I was about Amy, who seemed to have disappeared.

"Of course," Audrey said easily. "But you've had a morning. Why don't you sit down and rest a bit first? Are you sure you don't want that tea?"

I eyed her. She smiled back at me, but the expression seemed like something she'd pasted on. "Audrey, what's the big deal about the tea?"

Her eyes went very wide, and she nipped over and grabbed the bundle of my clothes. "I'll just go take care of these."

And if she did, would I ever see them again? "I'd rather you didn't do that."

"You can't wear them like this."

True. Nor did I have any way to make them presentable again. Except. "Leave the boots. I can deal with them if you've got some rags and maybe a little shoe polish. You'll get the rest back to me as soon as possible?"

"Oh, yes." She ducked out. I heard the front door close behind her as well.

I went over to the stove and lifted the teapot's lid. The contents steamed gently. I leaned over and sniffed at it. It didn't smell like anything much, but I've always been more of a coffee drinker myself – you can't really live in Seattle and not drink coffee or they'll kick you out of town – and what I know about tea isn't enough to tell whether somebody's trying to poison me or not. It didn't look lethal, though.

Still, I didn't think Audrey, or anyone else here for that matter, was trying to kill me. I lifted the pot, thinking to pour a little into a saucer and examine it further, when a voice came from behind me.

"Please put that down."

I nearly dropped the whole shebang, but managed to set it down without spilling anything. "Amy." I turned to see her standing in the doorway. She was back in her jeans and shirt that looked, I noticed now, kind of like my new clothes. Her shirt was pale green instead of black and her boots were light brown, though, not dark like mine. "How's Betsy?"

She smiled and came into the room. "Bouncing around and telling everyone all about her adventure." She went over to the stove. "You're a hero, you know."

"Hardly." I watched as she picked up the pot full of tea, walked carefully over to the sink, and poured till the pot was empty. She started to manipulate the pump until I came up behind her and took over for her.

When the water started coming, she stuck the teapot under it and rinsed it out thoroughly, then did the same to her hands. "That's enough, thanks."

I stopped pumping and eyed her. "What's with the tea? Or is that something else you're not supposed to talk about?"

She was silent for a moment, then changed the subject. Again. "Audrey said you looked handsome in your new clothes." She looked me up and down. "I have to say I agree with her." But she didn't look like she wanted to.

"Thank you. I think. I feel like a cowboy."

"I know. I felt that way at first, too. Like I should be out barrel-racing or something. But they're much better than the alternative, at least for me."

"What's the alternative?"

"I don't know what your alternative would be, but you saw mine last night."

Oh. "I take it you don't care much for dresses."

"I don't mind them every once in a while, but not every day." She didn't elaborate, but then she really didn't need to.

"I like you in jeans. They show off your, um–" I could feel myself turning red. Normally I wouldn't have had a problem complimenting a woman's ass or any other part of her figure, but Amy was different.

Or maybe not. She was laughing at me. "Thank you. It took some work to get that far with them – Belinda was shocked when I asked for trousers to begin with, and she wanted to put me in pants baggy enough to hold three of me, but I kept after her."

"Well, the results were worth it." There. That had to be a reasonable compromise.

"Thanks."

"But if you didn't like Belinda's efforts, why didn't you just go into Omak and get something there?" Oops.

Her eyes fell, but she actually had an answer for that one, for a change. "And hurt Belinda's feelings? I couldn't do that."

"I guess not."

She glanced back up at me. "There's going to be a dance Saturday night, at the old mercantile building, to celebrate – well." She hesitated, but went on before I could ask the obvious question. "Some of us are going over this afternoon to set up and maybe decorate a little. Would you like to come?"

That sounded – interesting. Well, not really, but wait. "The old mercantile building? Is that where the pig was?"

She gave me one of those grins that almost knocked me back a step. "Yes."

Well. Maybe I would have the chance to do some detecting after all. "Then I'd be glad to help."

* * *

That afternoon I headed back out, watching my step on the creaky porch. I still couldn't get past how different the little building looked on the inside than the outside, but – it looked like someone had been at work. For one thing, the broken porch board, where I'd nearly fallen through, had been replaced.

Actually, it looked like it hadn't ever been busted in the first place. The whole porch was in better shape. Oh, the boards were still silvery where the paint had worn off – paint? It hadn't been painted before. I shook my head and stepped down onto the ground. Anyway, the boards were smoother. Not as worn and buckled.

When I got to looking more closely, the whole town appeared that way. Not that freaky vision I'd had of it the other day? or was it this morning? Not like it must have looked in its heyday, with people bustling down its streets and fresh paint and unbroken windows. Just, better somehow. Like somebody cared. It made me glad. I didn't know why, and I didn't want to know why.

People seemed glad to see me, too. Which made me stop for a moment. There were *people* on the street. Not many. But a few. And they were folks I hadn't seen before. How many people lived in this place out in the back of beyond?

When I'd first arrived here, I'd thought I'd seen a crowd at my window peering in at me. Still, I'd been pretty out of it at the time. But some of the strangers' faces I was seeing here in Conconully this afternoon were vaguely familiar. Including that lady who'd been up in the tree. I made a mental note to see if Amy had permission to tell me who she was and why she'd been up there in the first place.

Although I've got to say what really mattered was how friendly everyone was. Every single one of them smiled, called me by name and had something nice to say.

By the time I reached the Mercantile Building, where Amy was waiting out front for me, I knew I was grinning like an idiot. Why do people always say that? Grinning is not idiotic. It feels good. People ought to do it more often.

She seemed to like the expression on my face, anyway, because she grinned back at me. "Ready to play Hardy Boys?" she asked me.

I couldn't help it. "You don't have the right equipment."

She took my hand. "We'll improvise. I'll be Nancy Drew." Her fingers were cool, and wrapped themselves around mine. If I wasn't careful, this grin was going to split my face.

"Um, Amy?"

"Yes?" She tugged me toward the door.

"I'm glad you don't have the right equipment."

She laughed out loud at that, and with her free hand yanked open the door.

It squonked, but not as badly as I'd thought it would. It led into a narrow hallway, walls on either side blocking access to the big bow display windows as well as the light pouring through them. The farther back we went, the darker it got, until by the time she threw open another door at the end of the hall, I had to put my free hand out against the rough planks so I could feel where I was going.

My first impression of the room on the other side of the door was that I'd walked into a cross between a cavern and a school auditorium. Our footsteps echoed on the smooth wooden floorboards and bounced back from a ceiling that had to be thirty feet up and walls I couldn't even see in the gloom.

"Hey!" Amy yelled, her voice reverberating in the empty space. "Why haven't you lit the lamps? Some of us can't see that well in the dark, you know."

The room sprang into light. Well, not exactly. It wasn't like they'd set up klieg lights in there. Or even a good set of track lighting. But the contrast between the gloom and the warm glow of a couple dozen – were those propane torches?

"Gas jets," Amy said, glancing up at me. "The latest thing for lighting back in the day."

"Why don't you guys at least get electricity?" I half expected another deflection or change of subject, so I answered my own question. "Don't tell me. The power company won't run lines this far back into the boonies."

"Pretty much."

"Then where's the gas coming from?"

"It's local." She ran out into the middle of the enormous room and spun around, her arms outstretched. "I love this space. It's so full of possibilities."

"What did you have in mind this time, Doc Amy?" I didn't recognize the speaker, who watched her from a far corner, sounding amused. He was short, was all I could tell, since the gas lights didn't reach quite back to where he was standing. Maybe a few inches taller than Amy, which wasn't saying much, and kind of stout.

"Oh, I don't know, Max." She stopped twirling around and looked at me. "What do you think, Danny?"

Danny? Nobody'd called me Danny since my mother left. I had no clue what she was talking about, and my face must have showed it, because she laughed, ran back to me, and took my hand. "Let's go see what's in the storeroom this time."

This was a whole new Amy, and I had to say I liked the transformation. I let myself be dragged over to one of the front corners of the room, where a door looked like it hadn't been opened in decades.

Amy tugged at the handle. It didn't give. "Max," she said, "quit that."

I looked at Max, who was just standing there in the shadows, radiating smugness somehow. Was this the man Amy had to get permission from?

"Max," Amy said again, in an exasperated tone.

"Looks like you need some help," he told her.

Amy froze, and gave him a hard look. "No, Max."

"What's going on?" I demanded.

"Max," Amy said carefully, "is being a twit." She shook her finger at him. "It's not the first time, nor will it be the last." She looked around the room, as if expecting agreement from the empty air.

Behind us, the door we'd come through opened, the sun gleaming across the wooden floor to Max's corner. Amy relaxed. The little man pouted. There really wasn't another word for it. It looked silly on his lined face.

"You're late!" Amy yelled to the newcomers.

"You really like making this room echo, don't you?" I said.

She nodded vigorously. "Oh, yes. Isn't it great?"

"I can't say I'm particularly fond of it, no."

"Spoilsport." But it she didn't seem to care.

As the group walked across to us, I noticed their footsteps didn't echo, like Rob's.

"I need some help here," Amy told them decisively. "We need the decorations, and Max here is being obstructive."

A tall young woman asked, "What would you like us to do with him?" Her hair was so dark it gleamed blue-black in the gaslight, and her eyes glinted with mischief.

"You probably don't want to ask me that."

"Couldn't Sheriff Dan help you?" asked a middle-aged woman. "Or did you ask him?"

"Cute, Peg," Amy said.

"You know, I *am* standing here," I said, and went to the jammed door.

"Don't!" It went up as a chorus. Even Max looked appalled.

"Oh, right. So, who's going to tell me I don't have permission to know why on this one?"

There was a lot of shuffling and looking away. I looked at Amy. She was examining her boot toes. For dust, apparently. There wasn't much of it. I waited. The whole group waited.

At last Amy muttered cryptically, "He's not ready for this." Which made no sense, since *she'd* been about to open the door herself.

I grimaced. "Okay, I'll bite. What the hell's behind that door?"

A small collective gasp went up. Amy glared at me.

I rolled my eyes. "Sorry. But, honestly, what's back there that's got you all so spooked?"

At that Max laughed. The sound bounced hollowly in the cavernous space, but it seemed to break the tension.

Amy sighed. "Dan, will you help me get this door open, please?"

I could too get answers from these people if I tried hard enough. "I thought you'd never ask."

CHAPTER 10

After all that discussion, it didn't take that much effort. The door wasn't nailed shut. The hinges worked just fine. I'm not even sure why Amy hadn't been able to get it open without me.

And when I did get a good hold on the tarnished brass doorknob and the big door swung wide, what was behind it was pretty anticlimactic. Cool, but anticlimactic.

The room behind the door apparently served as the storehouse for enough decorations to wrap up the entire town. Piles and bags of crepe-paper streamers and big, round Asian-looking lanterns and critters of all descriptions made out of honeycomb paper like those folding pumpkins my mother used to set around at Halloween. Bright colors shining against the dimness, and even some metallic stuff sparkling in the gaslight.

I glanced over at Amy, who looked pleased enough, and at the others, who were already pulling the big bags out and strewing their contents across the ballroom floor.

I leaned way over to get close to her ear. "Do you think the pig's in here?"

She shook her head. "No. That would be too easy."

"You think someone's playing hide and seek with it?"

She shrugged. "What else could it be?"

"Teenage vandals," I began, but she was shaking her head again.

"No, not here. They know they wouldn't be able to get away with it."

"The two aren't mutually exclusive."

"Hey!" called Max. "Aren't you two here to help?"

"Hold your horses, Max," I said, but Amy had already headed into the storeroom. I followed, and she shoved a bag of streamers into my hands.

"Go on. Let's get this done and get them out of here."

I grinned. "Gotcha."

She smiled up at me. "I've missed—" She bent back down to sort through more stuff. "Go on. I'll be out in a minute."

I thought about asking her what she'd missed, then decided not to. She probably wouldn't tell me, anyway.

* * *

The room was already beginning to look like someone was going to have a party. I was a bit dubious about the combination of gas jets and paper decorations, but nobody else seemed to be concerned, not even Amy, and I had to admit the effect was pretty elegant, considering what we'd started with.

Max produced a ladder from behind the stage, and I found myself attaching crepe-paper streamers to hooks high on the walls and throwing the rolls down to be caught by Peg, who tossed them back up to me after I'd moved the ladder across the room to the next hook. It looked like a multicolored spider web had taken over the ceiling. The final touch was the huge paper globe I placed at the point where all the streamers crossed.

I looked down from my perch at Max, who was, at my request, holding the ladder steady for me. "That work?"

Instead of answering me, he called across the room to Amy, who was creating a sort of bower over a cluster of wooden chairs in one corner. She raised her hand, her mouth apparently full of something, and waved, nodding her head at the same time. "I'd say that was a yes," Max said.

"I've got to agree with you." I started down the ladder, then stopped to look around.

It didn't look like the same place at all. Color and shape and movement had completely transformed the almost sinister-looking cave-like room into one ready for a good time.

Everybody was looking around, nodding with smug expressions on their faces. "Good," Amy said. "Looks like everything's ready. It's getting late. Time to close up." She began shooing everyone toward the front door.

Which went pretty well, till Max noticed she wasn't shooing me. He dug in his heels and glared at both of us. Amy glared right back at him. It was kind of like watching a teacup poodle stare down a gruff old terrier. The terrier might have thought he was winning, but the poodle thought she was a St. Bernard.

At last he shrugged and followed the rest of them out. The door closed behind them, and the gas jets wavered in the gust of air.

"It looks good," I told her. "Reminds me of my high school prom, sort of."

She nodded, all business now. "Well, that explains something, anyway." She headed toward the auditorium's stage.

"Explains what?"

"Never mind. Time to pig hunt, before Max comes back in here and chases both of us out. You start at that end, I'll take this one, then we'll meet in the middle."

"Okay."

She was already headed toward the heavy drapes blocking off everything but a foot or so of the raised platform. She ducked behind one end of the curtains, setting them swaying. I shrugged and did the same on the other end.

And I'd thought that storeroom was cluttered. If Amy thought we were going to make it through all those piles of boxes, heaps and rolls of fabric, and other, even stranger, detritus in one afternoon, she was crazy.

But it was fascinating. Like a treasure hunt. Full of odd things, everything from old clocks to an autoharp like the one my third grade teacher had played for us to sing to in class. Shoes and boots and boxes of buttons. Toys. Hand tools. I hefted an old hammer and thought about absconding with it in case the porch fell in on me again, then decided if I needed it I knew where it was. Nothing, I noticed, was modern. Even the sewing machine stuck in the far corner was an old-fashioned model with a treadle. But that didn't surprise me anymore.

No plaster pigs, though.

"Amy?"

"Hmm?" She didn't look up.

"Why couldn't you open the door to the storage room?"

"Oh, it was just stuck." But she sounded off, somehow. Like a suspect who wasn't telling the whole truth. And it hadn't been stuck. After Max had – given in? The door had opened as if the hinges were oiled.

"Then why did you tell Max to quit it? Quit what?"

Silence.

"Amy?"

But then I heard the door open. And footsteps. Lots of them.

And Amy certainly reacted then. "Come on. Quick."

She ducked around the curtain, and I followed, but we weren't fast enough. Standing in the middle of the wide-open floor were Rob, Audrey, Belinda, and Max. None of them looked thrilled with us. Belinda in particular had her arms folded across her ample chest and her face set in a frown.

"See, I told you," Max was saying. "In there making a mess."

"We weren't doing any harm," Amy said quickly. She looked up at me as if expecting corroboration, so I gave it to her.

"Not a thing. Just poking around a little." I added, as master of the obvious, "I could have spent days in there."

That was the wrong thing to say, apparently. But then most of what I said to these people tended to be the wrong thing.

"Did you move anything?"

Amy flinched. "I did not."

Belinda turned that glare on me. "Did you?"

I made it a point not to flinch. "Um, no, I don't think so."

"You don't think so."

Yeah, I was glad I'd left the hammer where it was. "I didn't take anything, if that's what you mean."

Audrey tugged on Belinda's sleeve. "I'm sure it's fine."

"Oh, I'm sure it's fine, too. And a fine thank you as well."

"Let's go." Rob headed back toward the door, his shoulders sagging.

"Yes, please," said Amy. She sounded as if she were about to apologize, but stopped short. She took my arm. I glanced down at her in surprise. "Humor me," she said softly.

"Sure." I wasn't about to complain about her clinging to me, especially when Audrey glanced over at us and the worry melted off her face.

* * *

I was left to my own devices that evening, which was fine with me. I wondered if Amy was standing up in front of some town tribunal being read the riot act for having ventured into an unauthorized storage room or something. I wouldn't have put it past Belinda to have organized one, and carried the thing through, too.

I supposed I should have gone to try to find out. But I'd probably have only made things worse. I guess I could see how maybe we shouldn't have been mucking around back there, but we really weren't doing any harm. Just looking for that damned pig, which hadn't been there, anyway.

I was pretty sure someone had made off with it. It was probably gracing the roof of one of the local schools right now. Or not. I'd seen the only truly local school on one of my strolls through town. It was just a couple of blocks from my house, and its roof was steep enough that balancing a three foot long, two foot high plaster pig on the ridgepole would have been quite a feat.

Somehow I didn't think these kids took the bus to Omak for high school, either.

I gave up on sleuthing for the night and went to bed.

* * *

Next morning after breakfast, courtesy of Audrey who didn't stay to keep me company while I ate, I dragged one of the wooden chairs out onto the porch so I could watch the world, such as it was, go by.

That world was busier than it had been when I'd first arrived. There were more people, for one thing, bustling or strolling past. Some waved at me, and I waved back. I wished I had somewhere to go.

You do, I reminded myself. Odd, how I'd let myself forget that finding my way out of here was what really mattered. I hadn't even tried in the last few days. And I was oddly reluctant to try now.

I got up anyway, carried the chair back inside, and pulled the door closed. Then, almost against my will, I set off down the street.

I hadn't gotten more than two blocks, having been nodded at by and nodded to at least half a dozen people, when young Tim snagged me. "Where ya' goin', Sheriff?"

I wasn't sure why I thought it probably wasn't a good idea to tell anyone I was trying to get out of here, but I said, "Just getting some exercise."

That earned me a wrinkled forehead, and a "Huh?"

"Stretching my legs."

"Oh." His forehead smoothed out. "Yours look like they're plenty long enough already."

I laughed, wondering why I was grateful the kid had distracted me from my purpose. "Why aren't you in school?"

His face fell. "We don't have a teacher. Not since Miss Clancy left."

Left?!? "Left?" I said, trying not to choke. "Where'd she go?"

The boy shrugged. Before I could try to drag anything else out of him, another voice I recognized called out from down the street. "Timothy James Fogle!" It wasn't his mother's but Belinda's. I wondered what she wanted with him, but he was already skipping away.

"Uh-oh. Gotta go. Nice talkin' with you, Sheriff."

He ran off. I stared after him. *Left?!?*

After a moment, I realized I was holding my breath, let it out, and set out down the street.

It was like some sort of fog had cleared from my brain. Like I'd just – forgotten – who I was and where I was supposed to be and what my responsibilities were and now all of a sudden I remembered. I'd been dawdling around here for how long, doing what? Okay, so maybe Betsy Fogle had needed me to get her out of that stupid well, but I wasn't the only person in town who could have done that.

My cruiser was out there somewhere. With any luck I could get the motor running and charge the radio back up at the very least, and then get some sort of signal through. There was a whole world out there, and that's where I belonged. Not in some half-cocked ghost town with a bunch of people who thought they were living in the nineteenth century.

I was clear out of town by the time I stopped for breath. I'd gotten really out of shape since I'd arrived here if a level walk of less than a mile could wind me. The weather had turned, and it was snowing out of a sullen gray sky, big fat flakes landing on my coat, my bare head, the tops of my boots. I shivered. The clothing I'd been given had seemed plenty warm when I'd put it on this morning, but it wasn't nearly enough to block that cold wind. I turned up my collar, but it didn't help.

My stomach growled. Hell, it hadn't been that long since breakfast, and I'd been eating better than I ever had in my life for the last – how long had it been? I didn't think it had been more than a few days, but I'd been losing track of time. Days, or weeks? I shoveled a hand through my hair, dislodging a fine skiff of snow.

Had they given up the search? Did anyone even care, or was I just another missing person by now? I didn't even know if I'd made the local news, since I hadn't been on the Internet since I'd gotten here.

Internet. Hell, even Amy didn't know what a cell phone was.

I sank down onto my knees, the wet snow soaking through my jeans as if they weren't even there. My wrist – the one I'd thought I'd broken, that had healed so quickly – started aching like a son of a gun. From the cold?

"What the hell are you doing out here, Reilly?" Not that anyone was here to answer. That was something else I'd forgotten. I hadn't felt this alone since – since I'd arrived here.

The chances of anyone ever finding me out here were about as good as me ever finding my stupid cruiser.

All I could think was, I have to get out. I have to get back. I have to...

I closed my eyes and sank down into the snow.

CHAPTER 11

"You young numskull." I groaned. I recognized that voice. It belonged to Rob. "What on God's green earth did you think you were doing out there?"

"Do you really think he's going to answer you right now?" That was Amy. My eyes popped open.

"Hey, he's awake."

"Damn right," I said, or tried to. My tongue was thick and cold. I attempted to lift my hand instead, which wasn't much more of a success.

"Hypothermia," Amy said decisively. "Among other things. He'll be fine once we get him warm again."

I felt like I already was.

"Stay still. Rob, sit on him or something."

A heavy hand came down on my chest. I tried to glare at him, but he wasn't looking at me. I tried to follow his gaze, but decided it was too much effort and closed my eyes again. I'm not going anywhere, I told him. Tried to tell him. The hand lifted. Another blanket came down on top of me, and I gave up on trying to stay conscious.

* * *

When I woke again, I felt fine. Like I'd had a really good night's sleep. My head was clear and I was warm all the way down to my fingers and toes. I stretched, luxuriating in how fantastic I felt, and at a chuckle, opened my eyes.

I swear, it was as if the past few days had never happened. Amy was perched on the wooden chair next to my bed, smiling at me. I smiled back.

"Feeling better, are you?"

"Yeah." I looked her up and down. "Thanks." I propped myself on my elbow. She didn't try to push me back down, which I took as a good sign.

The weariness on her face wasn't such a good sign. "What happened?"

"You don't remember?"

I thought about it for a minute, then shrugged. The blankets slipped down and I realized I didn't have anything on underneath. I fell back as I tried to grab onto them before they slipped away altogether. "Why am I naked?"

Her cheeks went a nice shade of pink, but she answered matter-of-factly, "Your clothes were sopping wet and you had hypothermia. Rob dealt with them," she added. "Your modesty is intact."

I felt myself blushing, anyway. "Oh." I did remember the cold. And the snow.

"What were you doing out there in the woods?"

As if she didn't know. "I thought I'd take a walk."

"Well, that was foolish of you." She stood.

"Where are you going?" Was that panic in my voice?

"You're not my only patient."

"Amy, who was Miss Clancy?"

She sat back down again. "How do you know about Miss Clancy?"

"Tim mentioned her. Said she'd been the schoolteacher here, until she left. Where did she go?"

Amy was silent for a moment, then said bluntly, "I'm going to strangle that boy."

"Why? Because he's the only person here who's willing to volunteer any information whatsoever?"

She sighed. "I suppose it must feel that way to you."

I propped myself back up on my elbows. "Yeah, it does."

"Well, Miss Clancy did the same thing you just did, except she died for it."

Whoa. "She went for a walk and–" I let the words hang there.

"She went searching for something that wasn't there anymore, got lost, no one could find her, and," she swallowed, "Max found her skeleton the following spring. He said it looked like she'd been mauled by a bear."

"Oh." I literally could not think of anything else to say. I scootched up to a sitting position, keeping a firm grip on the blankets, and put a hand on her arm. "I'm sorry."

Amy shook herself. "Well, as Max said when he told me about it, it was her own darned fault if she hated it here that much."

I pulled my hand back. "That's cold."

"So was she."

"I take it you didn't like her much."

"She was before my time. At any rate, her attitude had nothing to do with it, and I wouldn't wish getting mauled by a bear on my worst enemy." Then she put her hand on mine. "I truly wouldn't wish that on you. Please, don't go out there again. It's dangerous."

I thought about the outside world, and how I'd probably been given up for dead by now, anyway, and how it would freak everybody out if – when – I did make it back. "Not till spring, anyway."

She sighed. "Dan?"

"Yes?"

"It's never spring out there."

Before I could ask her what the hell she meant by that, she slipped her hand free and stood. "Now I really do have other patients. Even if I am just an EMT and not a real doctor, I'm all they've got here. You will rest and eat and behave today, won't you? I'll be back this evening to check on you. I'm sure you'll be fine by then."

"I feel fine now."

"I know." She put her hand on my forehead for a moment, then nodded. "Nice and warm, but not too warm. Good. Humor me today, okay?"

All of a sudden I was tired again, although I wouldn't have admitted it to her on a bet. I nodded back. "I'll humor you. Just for today."

"Thanks." And she was gone.

* * *

I slept for hours and woke in the late afternoon feeling rested again. I dressed in another set of clothes that had been left for me – I really needed to thank Belinda, whose handiwork it had to be – and went looking for food.

I found it, and Audrey, in the kitchen. She smiled at me as I came in. "Well, you're looking better. You've got color in your cheeks again. Looks like you may be able to talk Doc Amy into letting you escort her to the dance Saturday night, after all."

I grinned at her. "So I'm her date? Does she know that?"

Audrey rolled her eyes. "You mean you haven't asked her yet?"

"I, well, I, I hadn't thought–" I stopped before I landed flat on my face.

"You young men have all the courtesy of a bull in heat."

Christ, I thought. But she had a point. "I'll ask her tonight." I wondered nervously what escorting Amy to the dance was going to entail. A corsage? Meeting her folks? Oh, that would just be fantastic. Maybe she'd say no. That would get me off the hook.

Audrey must have found something amusing in my expression, because she laughed. At me, I was sure. Thanks, lady, I thought. She said tartly, "I certainly hope so. Now, I suppose you're hungry."

Before I could answer, my stomach growled. She laughed again. "Sit down."

I did.

* * *

Amy showed up just in time for dessert, which was some sort of incredible cake and cream production covered in caramel sauce. "Ooh," she said to Audrey, who smiled and dished up another serving without being asked. "My favorite."

Audrey smiled at her, then glanced meaningfully at me and said, "Well, I'll leave you two to it."

Amy picked up her spoon and scooped out a bite. "What did she mean by that?" Before I could answer she'd put the spoon in her mouth and I watched, fascinated, as her eyes closed.

I swear that dessert was making love to her mouth, judging from the expression on her face. She slid the spoon out slowly, her lips smooth around its bowl. She chewed, and swallowed, then, I guess realizing I hadn't answered her, opened her eyes. And blushed to the roots of her blond hair. "It's good," she said finally, scooping up another bite.

I shifted in my seat. "Yeah, I gathered as much."

"Why don't you try some yourself?"

Because I was having too much fun watching her? I picked up my own spoon and took a taste.

The dessert, like everything else I'd put in my mouth here, was delicious. I'm not sure it was orgasmic, the way Amy seemed to think it was. Obviously caramel was her thing. I'm more of a chocolate guy myself, but I sure was getting a kick out her enjoyment.

Finally, though, we'd scraped our bowls clean, and Amy said, "You never answered my question."

"What question?"

She gave me one of those 'I'm being patient with the clueless guy' looks. "What are we supposed to be doing?"

"I thought you were here to make sure I had a clean bill of health."

"Danny?"

"Why are you calling me that?"

"What?" she demanded.

"Danny. Nobody's called me that since I was shorter than you."

"Cute." She shrugged. "It suits you when you're being dense. And you're changing the subject."

"Am I?" It felt good to be frustrating her the way she'd been frustrating me.

She gave me a long-suffering look. It made me want to grin. "I can see from here you're back to your normal, aggravating self. So why did Audrey leave us all alone as if we had some private business to conduct?"

"Maybe she thought you'd want to examine me?"

"If that was the case she'd have fetched Rob."

"Why?"

"Propriety, my dear Danny. Propriety."

Oh, right. These people thought they were in the nineteenth century. I took a deep breath, wondered if I was about to put my foot in my mouth over 'propriety,' and said, "Would you like to go to the dance with me Saturday night?"

Her eyes opened wide for a second, then she looked away. "I should have expected it. Did Audrey put you up to this?"

And how was I supposed to answer her, stay truthful, and not tick her off all at the same time? "She mentioned it." Amy drew in her breath, but I kept going before she could say anything. "But I was already going to ask you. I don't want to go stag, and – you aren't seeing anyone else, are you?"

She let her breath out, and mine came out right along with it. "No, I'm not seeing anyone else. But I don't want you to feel like you're doing this just because you're supposed to."

"No," I said firmly. "No, I'm not. I'm doing it because, well, I like you. And I want to go to the dance, and I don't want to go alone." I hadn't realized till just then that I did want to go to this dance. Which was strange, and not just because I'd been trying to leave only when? This morning? Yesterday? The only dances I'd ever been to were Homecoming and my senior prom, neither one of which had exactly been fun occasions. More like nightmares, given that Homecoming had been the first time I'd ever gotten dumped, and the prom, well, let's just say getting drunk with a bunch of the guys and literally crashing the party had been an incredibly bad idea. It had come close to getting us all suspended, as a matter of fact, given Mickey Fields, his motorcycle, and what he'd done to the gym floor, not to mention the punch table, the band, and at least half the participants.

I snorted, then realized Amy was looking at me funny. "Just remembering the bad old days," I said.

113

"Oh?" A smile slid across her face, and I wondered if she had some bad old days in her past, too.

"So, will you go with me?"

"If you like."

"I do like. Do you?"

"Yes."

We sat there looking at each other for a bit after that. I don't know what she was thinking, but I was wondering how to ask her what the whole process entailed.

What I finally blurted out wasn't what I'd intended to ask. "When is Saturday, anyway? I don't even remember what day of the week I landed here."

Her lips quirked. "Today's Wednesday. You've been here for a little over two weeks."

"Wow. That long." Yeah, they'd probably quit searching for me by now. I wished I knew how I felt about that. I wished I knew how I was supposed to feel about it. It bothered me that I didn't feel – more, somehow.

She put a hand on my wrist. The one that had been aching so badly out in the cold. It wasn't aching anymore, thank God. "Is something the matter?"

"No. Yeah. I don't know."

"You know you're welcome to stay here as long as you like."

"Not that I'm not grateful to you and the whole damned town, but that's not the point." The sympathy – pity, more likely – on her face sent me straight into terminal ticked-offness. "The point is, apparently nobody out there cares that I just dropped off the face of the planet."

"How do you know that?" Yeah. Pity and patience. The last thing I wanted was anyone, but especially her, feeling that way about me.

"They've quit looking for me." She opened her mouth, but I kept going. "It's been two weeks. Trust me, they've quit looking for me."

"You did say they wouldn't have known where to look in the first place."

"Did I?" I stood up and paced across the kitchen and out to the porch. Amy followed me. It was a beautiful evening. Too beautiful for the end of November.

I stared up and down Okanogan Avenue, at the lamplight shining in the windows and the occasional passerby. "This place is strange." The understatement of my life.

Amy took my hand. It would have been rude to shake her off, so I didn't, but I wanted to. She felt sorry for me, that was all. I hated her feeling sorry for me

"No, it's not. It's a good little town, full of people who care about each other."

"And a bunch of secrets you won't tell anyone else. Are you ever going to tell me what's going on?"

"The very moment I can." She glanced up at the sky, as I looked down at her.

"Promise?"

"That is one thing I can promise you. With all my heart." She stood on tiptoe, her face tilted toward mine.

Did she want me to kiss her? Or would she slap me if I tried?

I bent, and took her face in my hands, my fingers in her soft gold hair, and kissed her gently on the lips.

CHAPTER 12

Well, she didn't slap me. As a matter of fact, when I was about to pull away, make it short and sweet, she reached up, put her hands on my shoulders and pulled me down closer, and kissed me back.

I hadn't quite expected that, somehow, but I sure wasn't complaining. I wanted to complain when she pulled away a few seconds later, though.

"Wait a minute," I said, as she stepped back. The pupils of her eyes were enormous, like she'd been smoking something funny, but I suppose it could have just been because it was getting dark out. I had no trouble seeing her, though.

"No," she said, a little breathlessly. "I need to leave now."

Maybe this was a nice little town, but that didn't mean she ought to be out alone after sundown. "I'll walk you home."

I remembered, vaguely, that I'd offered to do that once before and gotten freaked out by – something. I couldn't remember quite what.

"Oh," was all she said to that, but when I tucked her hand in my arm and stepped down off the porch, she didn't object. She seemed a little fuzzy-headed, as a matter of fact – the first time I'd seen the unflappable Amy in that condition. Not bad for just one kiss. Especially since it'd had the same effect on me.

We strolled down the street under the giant maple trees, past houses and shops and the Mercantile Building. I glanced up at it.

"Amy?"

"Yes?"

"Is anyone supposed to be in the Mercantile Building this time of night?"

She gave me a startled look. "No."

"There's a light in there." I put my other hand on her shoulder and turned her to look in the pigless window. "See it?"

"Oh." She seemed nonplussed for a moment.

Maybe whoever it was had Amy's pig. Or was trying to steal something else. "Look. I'm just going to check it out. You wait here."

"Dan, no—" Her voice trailed off as I tried the front door.

"Locked. Okay, I'll go around. I'm pretty sure I can get in the back. I mean it," I added when she started to follow me. "You wait here. Or go get help. Yeah, go get help." I headed around the back, into the dark and the weeds. "Go on," I called over my shoulder.

So far as I could tell, there wasn't anything worth stealing in there, but for all I knew Max could have had diamonds buried under all that rubble behind the stage curtain. Or, more likely, priceless antiques. Somebody obviously thought something was worth breaking and entering for, anyway.

There. I'd thought there'd be a loose latch. Somebody needed to put a better lock on this place. I slipped inside and tiptoed down the hall, breathing through my mouth for quiet and listening intently.

Except for the creaks and groans of an old building in the night, I couldn't hear a damned thing. It had dawned on me that whoever this was could be armed, but somehow I didn't think so. Was that the light again?

Maybe. I wished I'd brought a light of my own as I stumbled over something in the dark. I reached down. Was that the pig? It was about the right size, sort of vaguely rounded... Well, if it was, I could come back and get it later. I stepped around it, more carefully this time, and kept going.

I reached the door to the auditorium. This one opened out to the back of the stage. If I could get through all the crap without killing myself, maybe, just maybe...

I opened the door. It creaked. Of course it creaked. Nothing in this place had been oiled in a hundred years. I blinked. I thought my eyes had adjusted to the dark, but it was what I was seeing that made me want to rub my eyes and swear.

I did rub my eyes. And I did swear, silently so as not to warn the B&E. But when I opened them again, the half-gone roof, the timbers lying half-collapsed under the open sky, the grass knee-high where the floor should have been, were gone. And the building was as we'd left it – yesterday? Crepe-paper streamers, Japanese lanterns, and all.

I stood stock still, trying to get my bearings, listening with all my might. Nothing. Peered through the gloom. Nothing. No lantern bobbing around like some sort of will-o'-the-wisp.

Then a beam of warm lantern light shone through the door at the front of the building, and a voice called, "Dan? You in there, boy?"

Max. Of course.

"Yeah," I called, certain that if there had been anyone in here, he was long gone. "I'm coming. Hold your horses."

* * *

"So, all in favor say aye."

The ayes reverberated around the room.

"All opposed say nay." Rob sounded like he'd come after anyone who said nay personally, but the silence was resounding.

I sat on the stage in the auditorium I'd been investigating. There was some sort of irony in it, but it was probably the only room in town big enough to hold everyone. The room was packed beyond fire codes as it was, I thought, staring out at what seemed like a sea of faces. Most of them were old enough to be my parents. Some were old enough to be my grandparents.

I hadn't realized this many people lived in this place. There had to be almost a hundred of them. And every single one was smiling at me. Even Max, who had not been amused to find me "bulling around in here knocking everything over" last night, had forgiven me when I'd told him what I'd seen.

"You're playin' sheriff, boy, chasin' after criminals and rescuing people, you might as well take it on all official-like."

"You guys have rescued me more times than I've rescued any of you," I'd told him. "And I'm not qualified."

But all he'd said to that was, "You tell that to Betsy Fogle's mother."

So he'd told Rob, and word had gone out, and the next thing I knew here I was, sitting in front of the entire town of Conconully getting voted in as sheriff. It was a helluva promotion from lowly state trooper, I had to admit.

"We haven't had a sheriff in a while," Rob said now. "Not sure we're going to know what to do with one."

Amy, on my other side because I'd told her I'd rather be freezing to death out in the woods again if I had to go through this by myself, said in a clear strong voice, "I know what you're all going to do. If anything goes wrong, you're going to fetch Sheriff Dan Reilly. And he's going to help you set it right."

The applause startled me. It wasn't like I'd done a damned thing yet except needing to be rescued. But it was a vote of confidence if I'd ever seen one.

Amy was smiling up at me. I shook my head at her. "Who *are* you people?"

She put a hand to her ear. "What?"

"Never mind."

The applause was dying down. They were all looking at me like, oh, God, they weren't expecting some kind of speech, were they?

Amy nudged me. I looked over at Rob. He gestured me to stand up. I gulped and stood. The silence was so thick I couldn't get my breath.

"I, uh." I gulped for air. I'd been on the debate team in high school. This wasn't any worse than that. Really. "Thank you for your confidence in me. I'll try to live up to it. I, uh, will do my best to take care of whatever criminal activity may come Conconully's way, and to keep this town safe." There. That had to be enough. I sat down again as the applause broke out for a second time, and leaned over to Amy to say something directly in her ear so she couldn't possibly not hear me.

"You people are *crazy*."

She turned her mouth to my ear, close enough for me to feel her warm breath against it. "No, we're not."

I've never been slapped on the back so many times in my life. It was like they'd had the highest crime rate in the country and I was going to singlehandedly turn it around for them. I didn't have a chance to ask what had happened to the old sheriff. I didn't have a chance to go into the back room and see if what I'd stumbled over was Amy's pig, either, although I wanted to. I told Max, when he came up to congratulate me on my new job, that I was going to need

121

to examine the Mercantile for evidence of the break-in tomorrow, and he not only didn't object, but handed me the keys.

"You can get them back to me when you're done." He nodded decisively.

"Thanks." I hadn't thought it was going to be that easy.

"If I can't trust the sheriff, who can I trust?" He grinned at me and I ducked yet another thump. My shoulder blades were getting sore.

I decided not to mention the only thing separating the Dan he'd wanted to throw out of his building for poking around, from the Sheriff Dan he'd just handed his keys to, was the badge Rob had pinned on my shirt. It wasn't a cheap tin jobby, either, but sturdy, made of thick brass. But it was just a badge. I was still the same man.

"You can trust me," I told him, trying very hard not to laugh. The whole situation was unbelievable.

Your whole life is unbelievable, I thought. And then I did laugh. If this was unbelievable, I'd take disbelief over reality any day.

It wasn't until I'd walked Amy home afterwards, finally getting her all the way to her little house on the edge of town – the third time being the charm, apparently – that I realized I meant it.

I saw her in, copping another kiss before she closed the door, and started back toward my house. My house. I gazed around my town as I strolled back through the starlight. My house. My town.

I remembered what it had looked like when I'd first arrived, all tumbledown and weedy. How empty it had seemed. How could I ever have thought it was empty? Or sad?

This town was the most alive place I'd ever been. Which was exactly how I felt, too. I belonged here, as I'd never belonged anywhere before.

Maybe it was a good thing I'd never been found. So the folks back in the real world thought I was dead. That meant they weren't expecting to find me anymore. I suppose I should have felt guilty about not trying to let them know I was okay, but I had tried, and the second time could have killed me. I'd done my best. No one was going to miss me. Dad and Carol had quit missing me long before the accident. And Linda. I snorted. I wasn't glad she'd dumped me – I'm not that crazy – but well, I wasn't sure how else to describe how I felt just now.

I belonged here. These people wanted me here. I was just selfish enough to like that, a whole bunch. And then there was Amy...

I climbed the tidy white steps of my house. Wondered, for the first time, who owned it and who I needed to start paying rent to. Maybe I could buy it.

After all, I was the sheriff of Conconully. My new job had to pay more than my old one did.

Chapter 13

My first formal task as the real official sheriff of Conconully, Washington, began the next day when I went to investigate the Mercantile Building. I pinned my badge onto my shirt pocket and headed down the street, still not quite convinced I wasn't an imposter. Or maybe just faking it. Or both. But I did have law enforcement training, after all, and I had been voted in. Overwhelmingly, in fact.

Everyone I passed on Okanogan Avenue nodded at me and smiled, as they'd been doing ever since I arrived here, but their attitude was different. It wasn't like I deserved anyone's respect or anything, so I guess it was the badge.

I was determined to earn that respect, though, by finding out who'd broken into the Mercantile, and what they'd found there.

I let myself in through the front door with Max's key, and waited for my eyes to adjust to the relative gloom inside before I went on. There was just enough light that I could get away without trying to light the gas jets, which was a good thing. I'd probably have burned the building down trying, and that would be a heck of a way to start my new career. I made a note to get Max, or someone else, to show me how the whole rigmarole worked sometime.

I did wish I had a flashlight, though. But I could see well enough to notice there weren't any footprints in the front hall or marks on the walls. Which made a certain amount of sense. I doubted my culprit had entered through the front door, either. I unlocked the two side rooms backing up to the display windows and looked around. Nothing. Not around the windows, not – Wait a minute.

I examined the floor of the display window, which was raised from the floor of the room to about knee height. Just below where the missing pig had been was a recessed handle.

I let out my breath. Of course there'd be a handle. I wished I had a way to dust for fingerprints, but maybe there'd be some evidence under that trap door. That space would be perfectly good storage for window props and such. Or maybe something more valuable.

I used the bandanna Belinda seemed to think was a vital part of my wardrobe to grasp the handle and pull up. I half expected something to pop out and make me jump, but the only thing flying into the air was a cloud of dust. I waved the cloth, coughing, then peered down into the dark hole.

It wasn't just a little storage space under the window. A ladder leaned against the side of what looked like another well, only this one wasn't wet and slimy. I eyed the dimensions of the hole in the floor, which weren't big enough to allow me access to that ladder, and swore in frustration. What I needed was a saw. What I didn't need was how pissed off Max was going to be if I sawed up his display window floor. On the other hand, unless the B&E was built like a two by four, no way was he using that hole for anything, either. Not to mention the dust cloud. No, that mystery was purely curiosity, not crime-solving. Dammit.

I closed the trap door reluctantly, made a mental note to figure out some way to get down there at some point, and got back to work.

The other display window didn't have a trapdoor. So much for being able to get down there and crawl across.

The rest of the building was just about as disappointing. Not a single crepe-paper streamer had been disturbed, and even the stage's piles of stuff were about how Amy and I had left them, so far as I could tell. When I finally made my way back to the hallway leading to the rear entrance, what I'd thought might be the pig turned out to be an empty barrel lying on its side. I turned it on end and sat down on it, not feeling very useful.

So. What had I seen, when was it, night before last? Maybe I hadn't seen anything. The lights had seemed real. And Max had been willing to believe I'd seen something, although he hadn't been all that exercised about it.

Like he knew who it was, I thought suddenly. Like he knew and he didn't care. But why set me after whoever it was if he didn't care?

Well, I cared. I cared if he was laughing up his sleeve at me, if people felt like I needed busywork to keep me happy, if putting this badge on me was supposed to make me feel like I belonged or something.

The thing was, it hadn't felt like busywork till now. I locked the building up and went in search of Max. He could have his damned keys back and good riddance.

* * *

I finally caught up with him in the Gold City Saloon. I pushed through the genuine Old West style swinging doors to find him holding court, the center of attention in a small crowd as he told some story or another.

I shouldered my way through. "Kind of early to be drinking, isn't it?"

He laughed and waved his bottle, which had a label on it I didn't recognize. "Never too early for a good ale, son." He set it down on the bar, and turned back to his listeners.

I pulled the keys out of my pocket. "Don't you want to know what I found?"

I'd interrupted him in mid-sentence, which I think annoyed him, but he gave me his attention again.

"What did you find?"

"Not a damned thing."

He picked up his keys. "Well, then. Thank you for your time, Sheriff."

His reply annoyed me, but I had to ask. "Where does that tunnel go?"

He stared at me. "Tunnel?"

"The one underneath where the pig used to be."

"What on earth are you talking about, boy?"

"The tunnel. Underneath the trap door in the display window."

"There's no tunnel."

"Oh yeah?" I grabbed the bottle from where he was about to take another swig and thumped it down on the counter. "Come see." I grabbed his arm.

He shook me off. "Looks like I'm not the only one who's been drinkin', boy."

Now that was an insult, and I wasn't going to take it without a fight. "Come look, dammit."

He sighed. "You going to pester me till I do?"

"No." Oh, I could have. It didn't have anything to do with the supposed crime I was trying to solve. Or maybe it did. It was the principle of the thing. "No, I'm not."

"Then come on, boys. Let's go take a gander." He rose.

"You're bringing all of them?"

"Why not?"

I counted heads, looking for someone skinny enough to go down through that hole. Nope. Nope. Maybe. Definitely nope.

At least I'd have witnesses when Max saw the tunnel he was pretending didn't exist.

I led the way out of the saloon and down the block to the Mercantile Building, feeling like the Pied Piper.

Max unlocked the door. I shoved it open and headed straight toward the pigless window. I could feel the bodies crowding in behind us as I reached it and pulled the connecting door open.

I pointed. "There. Trap door."

"Yes. I see." Max sounded like he was trying to be bored, but he was grinning. I've never seen anyone enjoy being the center of attention as much as he did, but I didn't appreciate it right then.

I pulled up on the handle. Unlike the first time I opened it, it stuck. I yanked. It wouldn't open.

"Okay, this is weird. It opened right up before." I peered around the crowded room for the biggest set of shoulders, and pointed. "You. Come here, please."

A big man with a mustache that looked like it belonged on a Super Mario Brother pushed his way forward.

"Grab on," I told him.

He looked at Max, who nodded, grinning smugly.

The fellow got a grip, and so did I.

"One, two, three," I said, and we both pulled. The trap door creaked. Almost there. I glanced up just in time to see Max frown in concentration.

Then I caught on. "All right, Max. Enough funny business." Whatever the hell it was.

Max looked affronted. "I beg your pardon?"

"I bet you do." I frowned myself, thinking about the other day, and Amy's comment about Max and the door to the decoration room. "So, who's got to do what to get this door open?"

He shrugged. "How would I know?"

"It's your building, Max," said a voice from the back. It sounded like Rob, and he sounded annoyed, for some reason. "You can't have it both ways."

Max scowled.

I waited, making eye contact with the behemoth next to me. He tightened his grip.

Max sighed. "Try it now."

We yanked, and I for one nearly landed on my butt. The door whanged back against the raised floor of the bay window with a hollow-sounding clunk. I regained my equilibrium as the dust settled, and peered in.

The tunnel was gone.

Chapter 14

A few hours later I was sitting on my front porch, still trying to decide when, exactly, I'd been hallucinating. Was it when I'd seen the tunnel, or when I'd made an absolute fool of myself by trying to show my imaginary tunnel to Max? Was he hiding something – the first thing that sprang to my mind was illegal drugs, but – here? We weren't all that far from the Canadian border. BC Bud marijuana, and worse, had been smuggled down across the border for decades.

About ten years ago, back before marijuana was legalized, when I'd been in junior high and wanting to be a cop even back then, I'd seen a story on the television news about a tunnel, several hundred yards long, smugglers had dug from a barn on a border-hugging farm, stretching to another outbuilding on a border-hugging farm on the other side. When the border patrol discovered and raided it, the tunnel had been full of bales of marijuana, ready for shipment further south. It was one of the biggest drug busts ever in the state of Washington at the time.

But for one thing, we were a lot farther from the Canadian border than a few hundred yards. More like twenty or thirty miles, as the crow flew, which was way too far for a tunnel. For another, marijuana is legal in the state of Washington these days, although the drugs didn't have to be marijuana. But I couldn't quite see even Max as a drug smuggler. Besides, if he was, he'd have found a way to keep me out of the Mercantile Building in the first place.

But if he hadn't known...

Oh, he knew. Somehow I was more than sure he knew that tunnel existed. But where did it go and what was hidden down there?

And how was I going to find out? I wondered what the chances of him giving me permission to case his building again were, and if they were any better than a snow cone's in hell.

I don't need his permission, I thought. Yes, I did. I was the sheriff, but without his permission I needed a search warrant. Unless...

I still didn't need his permission. Or, rather, I'd have it again soon. I could feel the smile growing. The dance was Saturday night. The whole building would be thrown wide open. If I couldn't sneak away and figure out what was going on then, I probably should turn that badge right back in.

* * *

It wasn't until the next afternoon that my services as sheriff were called upon again, and then it was for something I'd have called animal control for in my other life.

I didn't recognize this breathless kid. He was probably about eight, towheaded and scruffy in overalls and boots and a canvas jacket, and he stood panting when I answered the door.

"What's the problem?"

It took him a second to get the words out, his eyes huge and round. "Wolf. Rabid wolf."

"What? Where?"

"Out by the schoolhouse." He grabbed my hand. "Come on."

What the hell was I supposed to do about a rabid wolf? "How do you know it's got rabies?" For that matter, how did he know it was a wolf, and not just somebody's dog, or even a coyote?

"It's foaming at the mouth. And it's blocking the door. Nobody can get out."

"How did you—"

He interrupted me. "They boosted me out the back window and I ran before it saw me. Sheriff." He was practically dancing in place.

"I'm coming, I'm coming." I wasn't sure I believed him. We do have wolves in eastern Washington. They're rare, but they do drift down from Canada sometimes. Hell, even bear sightings are a rite of spring in Seattle. We've got wilderness by the square mile here, and when you get wilderness, you get critters.

But a rabid wolf? Right here in town? It was probably somebody's dog, and – so how could I explain the foaming at the mouth thing? Exaggeration. Or maybe it had a bone caught in its teeth. It wouldn't be the first time.

I wished I had my gun, though. What the heck this kid expected me to do about this so-called rabid so-called wolf was a bit beyond me right now.

The kid, whose name was Brian, insisted I sneak up on the schoolhouse, which was up on a rise at the end of Wauconda Street, set back from the rest of town, from behind. He wanted to come with me, but I made him stay put a good distance away, and began mounting the hill slowly and quietly through the grass and brush toward the back of the little white building, trying to figure out a way to get everyone out safely without the critter seeing us.

That idea died a quick death when I heard the growl. That wasn't anybody's dog. Or even a coyote. It was too full-throated. My breath jammed in my lungs and I had to make a deliberate effort to get it loose again.

I couldn't see the wolf right away. The blackberries were pretty dense around the schoolhouse, and it was hard to get a clear line of sight. I was about to try to edge my way a bit closer, every grain of my attention on the situation at hand, when someone tapped me on the back.

It was about all I could do not to yell. I clamped my mouth shut and turned around.

"Here." It was Amy, and she was holding out a gun. An antique pistol, for God's sake. I wondered wildly where the hell she'd gotten it.

"Where the—" We were both whispering, but she put her finger to my lips and held the thing out to me.

"It's loaded."

I wanted to strangle her, but I didn't have time just now. I'd interrogate her about that later. I took the gun and checked. Yup. Fully loaded. Except for the chamber under the hammer, which, thank God, was empty. I wondered if it would fire when I pulled the trigger or blow up in my hands. "Thanks. Now get out of here before it sees you."

"Yes, sir." She slipped away, down the hill toward town, and I turned back to my job, feeling some better, at least with deadly force in my hands. Such as it was. What I wanted was my un-smashed service revolver, but this was going to have to do.

I edged my way to the back window and tapped on the glass. Immediately several faces popped into view, and the sash slid up. They were all kids, dammit.

I put a finger to my lips, touching where Amy had touched them just a moment before. "Is there an adult in there with you?"

"No, sir," came a whispered chorus.

Of course not. "Okay. Stay quiet, stay calm, and whatever you do don't try to open the door or climb out the window until I give you the all clear."

The growl came again. The window went down with a slam. I turned around.

All I could think was, oh, shit, it really is a wolf.

I'd be willing to bet it had been a glorious animal in its prime, but it sure wasn't now. Its ribs showed through its tattered gray coat, and one of its feet was dragging as if it had escaped from a trap at some point in its past. What fur it did possess was full of burs and twigs, and its eyes were more than just the normal wild of the wolves I'd seen before on visits to Northwest Trek when I was a kid. It was hurting, maybe dying, and it hadn't had a good meal in I don't know how long.

And, yes, it was foaming at the mouth. Rabies or no rabies, that was one sick animal. I'd be doing it a favor to put it out of its misery. The thought made my stomach churn, anyway.

Slowly I raised the Colt, hating to have to depend on a firearm I hadn't tested. Carefully I aimed it. The animal stood stock still, staring at me, as if it had never seen a human with a gun in its life. For all I knew it hadn't. I could hear its breathing, see its lungs make its ragged sides bellow in and out. It growled again.

I gulped. Steadied my aim at its head. Prayed to whatever gods were out there to forgive me. And fired.

The recoil didn't knock me off my feet, but I think that was more because I'd overdone bracing myself for it. The kick still jolted me back some.

I swear I saw surprise in that poor animal's eyes as the bullet struck it. The force made it jerk, and it fell into the grass. I took a careful step forward. Two. Three. And I was standing next to it.

I stared down at the sad corpse. Point blank range or no point blank range, I'd been damned lucky to kill it with the first shot. I nudged the head with my foot, watching its blood stream onto the ground. I'm a good shot, have been ever since I first set foot on a firing range, but to hit it straight in the eye like that, on the first shot – well. I shook my head, not sure I believed it myself.

"Sheriff! Sheriff!" High-pitched, excited voices. They were outside, and getting closer. I left the dead wolf where it lay, and aimed myself toward the front of the school to head the kids off.

"Hey!" I said as they surrounded me a moment later. "What did I tell you about staying put till I gave you the all clear?"

"But we heard the shot! Did you get him? Where is he? Was he rabid?" I was outnumbered and surrounded. I kept going toward the front of the school, and sat down on the step. The kids ganged up around me.

"Just because you heard the gun fire once doesn't mean he's dead," I told them sternly. "Yes, I got him. He's back there – no, stay here, you don't need to be messing with a dead animal, especially since I don't know if he's got rabies or not."

I looked up as Amy came around the corner. Her expression was somber. "I can't be sure, either, but I think he might have." She nudged a couple of the kids away, and sank down beside me. "Thank you. That could have been much worse."

I hoped she wasn't about to be sick. I put an arm around her, wanting the support myself, and examined the pistol thoroughly for the first time. A Colt Peacemaker, I was pretty sure. Damn. I wondered how much it was worth. In the outside world, plenty, but here? I snorted and Amy tilted her head back, smiling. She rolled her eyes at me, obviously in on the joke.

But it wasn't a joke. As far as I was concerned, that probably priceless antique had just saved a whole bunch of lives. What it was worth out in the real world didn't matter. Gingerly, I set it down on the step. A couple of the older kids grinned at me, and one made to pick it up. I glared at him and he stepped back. "You all don't need me to tell you to go home. Do any of your parents know where you are?"

That got their attention. The group broke up, and I watched them as they straggled down Wauconda Street. Amy tried to stand, but while I wasn't about to admit I was still feeling the reaction to shooting that poor animal, I wasn't ready to let her go, either, so I tightened my hold around her shoulders.

She looked up at me. "One of us should go along and make sure they get home all right."

I snorted. "What, you think there's a pack of rabid wolves and not just one? I have to say I disagree with you."

"No, no." Her shoulders sagged, and I snugged her closer.

"That poor thing looked like it hadn't had a pack to run with for a long time. I imagine it got kicked out after whatever happened to its foot."

She sighed, and snuggled under my shoulder, her hair tickling my chin. My own adrenaline was subsiding now, and I relaxed just a bit at the comfort of having her there.

After a moment she leaned back and looked up at me again. I was about to cop a kiss when she said, "I meant it when I said it could have turned out much worse. Last year–"

I interrupted her. "This has happened before?"

"Every–" she cut herself off. "Yes. And this time, because of you, no one died. The last time we didn't have anyone who could handle it the way you did, and two children were bitten. Rabies is an ugly way to die."

I thought about the wolf, and the way it had stared me down. "It is." I hesitated, but – "Died?" I knew the answer to my next question, but I had to ask it, anyway. "You couldn't get them to the hospital for the shots?"

She just shook her head, and cuddled closer.

"Why?"

She sighed.

"Yeah, right." I scooted up, taking her with me, and leaned back on the doorjamb. Something about this place and all its secrets was beginning to make sense. But it wasn't a sense I liked one single bit.

CHAPTER 15

Of course there was a big hullabaloo when the story got out.
I've never seen so many pies and cakes and trays of cookies in my life.
It seemed like every time I turned around there was someone else at
the door with more.

I stared at Amy in consternation. "What am I supposed to do
with all this stuff?"

"Bring it to the dance?" she suggested. "Or I suppose you
could try to eat yourself sick, but I'm not sure what that would
accomplish."

I turned my attention to more important matters, and hefted
the Colt again, which I had to admit felt good in my hand. It was a
gorgeous piece of workmanship, and it had just saved my life, not to
mention Amy's and the lives of those kids. "Where did you get this?"

She hesitated. "It belonged to your predecessor."

I suspected I didn't want to know, not that it was likely she'd
give me an answer, anyway, but I had to ask. "What happened to
him?"

Her gaze fell, and she hesitated.

"Don't tell me, you can't –"

She smiled sheepishly. I groaned. "Great." I let it go. Again. "What day is it, anyway? I keep losing track."

"Does it matter?" She sounded genuinely interested. And genuinely relieved.

"I'm just wondering if all these goodies–" I picked up a cookie and bit down on it. Cinnamon and ginger exploded on my tongue. When I sighed this time it wasn't because I was ticked off. I chewed and swallowed. "Are they going to go bad by the time this shindig actually happens?"

Amy started to answer, but yet another knock on the door interrupted her. It wasn't more food this time, thank goodness, but Rob. He came in and looked bemusedly at the loaded table. "I hope you've got a sweet tooth."

He'd caught me with my mouth full. I swallowed again. "It would take half a dozen people who didn't care what their dentists said to take care of all this."

He laughed. "We'll think of a better way to pay you next time."

That stopped me for a bit. This was my pay? Well, it wasn't like I didn't have a roof over my head and three square meals on the table every day. I didn't even have to do my own cooking, or cleaning, or laundry. And it wasn't really like there was anywhere to spend cash money.

Rob was watching me. "Yes, the house is yours, and Audrey and Belinda are happy to do for you. Think of this as your bonus." His eyes became serious. "For risking your life for us this afternoon."

"He's bound and determined to make a hero out of himself," Amy said.

"Well, he's accomplished it, so far as we're concerned."

One of these days I really was going to have to pull an "aw, shucks, twern't nuthin," routine on them. Right now, though, all I wanted to do was sink through the floor.

"Not a hero," I said. "I just want to be useful." Not that being appreciated wasn't nice.

"Well, I hate to pull you away again so soon, but I thought you ought to know. People are talking about Harry Tracy again. Some say he's been seen in the woods outside town."

I heard Amy's indrawn breath.

"Who?" I asked.

"Oh, that's right, you wouldn't have heard," Rob said easily. "Harry Tracy's a bad piece of work. Folks call him a bandit, and that's true so far as it goes, but what he is amounts to is much worse than that."

"They say he's murdered a man," Amy said softly.

Rob nodded. "In cold blood, right on the main street of Molson, about six months ago."

"Why?" I asked.

"Nobody knows for sure. Got into an argument and decided to settle it with his six-shooter, from what it sounds like. It's happened before." He fell silent.

Okay. Not that people didn't settle arguments with guns in the 21st century. They did it every day, sometimes from their cars, even. But that was the first time I'd ever heard anyone refer to a gun as a six-shooter without cracking a smile.

"So, if this is a regular occurrence–" I began.

Both Amy and Rob interrupted me simultaneously. "No, it's not," she said indignantly, as Rob said, "Not in the back, it's not."

"Wait a minute. This Tracy guy shot his victim in the back?"

Rob nodded.

"And that's what's got you guys all worried?"

They both nodded this time.

"Did he have a beef with the victim?"

Rob shrugged. "He must have."

"Okay. So, yeah, he should be in prison for murder and I can see why you're all freaked out," I said. "Why isn't he?"

"Nobody's been able to catch him," Amy said. "Nobody's been willing to try."

Oh, no, you don't, I thought. I stared at her. "I thought you didn't want me to be a hero."

"I don't." But she said it too quickly.

Rob added, "No, we don't. And we don't want you trying to be one, either. That's a job for the marshals, and they're after him. Have been for months, and not just for the murder. He's wanted for train robbery and holding up banks, too."

"You mean like Butch Cassidy and the Sundance Kid?" Now I wanted to laugh, but both of them were nodding at me, solemn as owls, although Amy's eyes looked like she was having a hard time maintaining the expression.

I desperately needed to get Rob out of here and pin Amy to the wall about all this. Which was not a good metaphor, as an image of me physically pinning her to the wall sprang into my mind, me leaning into her, her leaning into me...

Harry Tracy. Right.

"Yes," Rob was saying. "And just about as dangerous."

"Okay. Well. Thanks for the warning. I will do my best to keep this town safe, and right now I need to figure out my strategy." I began to nudge Rob toward the door. He looked startled, but went.

When he was gone altogether, I turned to face Amy, who looked like she wished she'd gone with him.

"Butch Cassidy, Amy? Really?"

I had to give her points for trying to hold onto that solemn face, I really did, but as I watched her, the expression slipped, and we both busted out laughing.

142

By the time it ended I *was* holding her against the wall, although it was more to keep both of us from collapsing on the floor than anything else. I leaned into her, just like I'd imagined, but when she didn't lean against me in return, I pulled back a little.

She looked worried, not aroused. I sighed, took her by the hand and led her over to the table.

"It is serious, Danny," she said, settling herself into the chair I held for her. "I've heard stories about Harry Tracy. The murder's really the least of it. He's terrorized the Okanogan country for years."

"The name sounds sort of familiar, for some reason."

She smiled, but there was a hint of melancholy in it. She opened her mouth, but for once I thought I knew what was going on. I held up a hand. "Wait."

She did, watching me as I put two and two together.

"I read this book when I was a kid," I said slowly. "It was called *Outlaw Legends of the Pacific Northwest*." As she just watched me, saying nothing, I felt compelled to explain. "I wanted to be a cop, even back when I was a kid. I read all sorts of stuff about bad guys, anything I could lay my hands on. Anyway," I added, "that's not the point. The point is, Harry Tracy was in that book.

"But the thing is, Amy." I stared right at her. "He died in 1894."

The silence felt like lead. I couldn't have broken it if my life depended on it, even if suddenly it felt like it did.

Amy didn't look shocked, as I'd sort of expected her to. I couldn't get a bead on what she was thinking, to be honest. Finally, she said brightly, "Well, that's good to know."

I wanted to wring her neck. Not for the first time, I realized. "So. Are you finally going to tell me what the hell's going on here?"

* * *

Of course she didn't. It was a conspiracy. There's not a single doubt in my mind. But just as she opened her mouth, probably to tell me again she would as soon as she got her damned permission, a knock loud enough to sound like a battering ram pounded on my front door.

I swear I almost put my head through the ceiling.

"Hold your horses!" I shouted as we both headed for the door. I beat Amy there, but not by much, and I put out my free arm to keep her behind me as I opened it.

"Oh. It's you again. Dammit, Max, you don't need to knock my door down."

"He's here," Max said in an awed tone.

"Who?" I demanded.

"Harry Tracy. He's in my building."

"In the Mercantile? How the hell did he get in there?"

"The tunnel. He came in through the tunnel."

I barely managed to keep myself from decking him. "The tunnel you swore wasn't there? The one you used to make me a laughingstock of in front of half the town?"

He didn't even have the decency to look apologetic. "Sheriff, are you going to do something about him or not?"

"I ought to say 'or not,' and watch and see what you'd do," I told him, conscious of Amy no longer trying to get past my arm. No longer there at all, actually.

Max sagged visibly, then took a deep breath. It was like watching him inflate himself, as he drew himself up to his full height, which from my perspective wasn't very tall at all. "Thank you, Sheriff, for your considered opinion." He put a spin on the word sheriff that made it sound like he was saying bastard instead.

The smarmy little know-it-all jerk. "I told you what I ought to say, not what I'm going to do," I said, and watched the disdain on his face morph into disbelief. He opened his mouth.

I beat him to it. "Who saw him? When? Where in the Mercantile Building was he last seen? Does he have any firearms on him?"

"What do you think?"

"I think if you want me to catch him, you'll tell me every detail you know."

"While he ransacks the building?"

"You got more than two minutes worth of details?"

Max rolled his eyes, but at least he answered me. "Yes, he was wearing his holsters. Yes, I'm pretty sure they were full. He had a knife shoved into his belt, too."

"What else?" I demanded.

He shrugged. "Nothing else I know of. Are you coming or not?"

I lifted my gaze beyond Max to see a dozen or so faces, all male, all steely-eyed and determined. "Anybody else see anything?"

"He looked mad, Sheriff."

"Angry as hell, more like it."

"He have any, er , arguments with anybody here like he did in Molson?" I asked.

"Not unless you count—" a lone female voice – was that the tree lady? – in the back fell silent. Or was smothered.

"Not unless you count what?" I eyed Max, who was scowling and shifting from foot to foot.

He said nothing.

"You want my help, Max?" I asked. "If you do, you'll tell me anything, any little bit, that might help me. If not, you're on your own."

Max shifted his weight again.

"All right. Have fun." I backed up inside the doorframe and reached for the knob.

The words jerked out of him. "Tracy's wild because he's heard we've got a new sheriff."

I let go of the knob and stepped forward again. "That so?"

"Yeah."

"So this makes it personal, does it?" Personal? What stake did I have in this place? Besides everything that had happened in the last week? Month? Forever? I couldn't even remember how long ago I'd arrived here almost feet first and been rescued by these crazy people, and, oddly enough, it didn't matter. This was my town, these were my people, and even if I wanted to poke Max in the eye with a sharp stick, damned if I was going to let some stupid Butch Cassidy wannabe rob him or anyone else.

This was my town and I was its sheriff. Period.

"I need to get my gun." I turned and there was Amy holding my Colt out to me, and just when had it become mine?

"Thanks." I took it. She, or someone, had reloaded the gun. I tried not to think about the knife Tracy supposedly had. I'd been trained how to defuse knife fights, back at the academy, but that had been a long time ago.

At least that's how it felt.

From the table in the hall, Amy picked up something else and made to hand it to me. The thing looked like a big tin can corroded to black, only with a round, conical top. "You might want this, too."

Without thinking, I took it from her, conscious of Max giving her an approving nod. The can had a sort of bull's-eye made of glass set in the center of one side, a wire handle, and hinges and a latch holding it closed on the back.

I looked my question at her, but Max answered. "It's a dark lantern," he told me impatiently. "It belonged to the old sheriff. And yes, you're going to need it."

I shrugged, stepped out onto the porch, and addressed the men standing in the yard. "I want the Mercantile surrounded. Just in case he tries to get out instead of going back through the tunnel. Are you all armed?" A sea of nodding heads. "Good. Shoot to stop him, not to kill, unless it's kill or be killed. We want him to stand trial for everything he's done."

Another round of nods, accompanied by unconvinced expressions this time. As long as they did what I asked, they could be as dubious as they wanted. I turned to Max. "Show me the other end of that tunnel."

* * *

Well, I thought, isn't this just fascinating. I'm not sure where I'd expected the other end of the tunnel to be, or what I'd find there, but I'd half expected a still, or a marijuana grow operation, or something that would have been illegal back whenever these people thought they were. Did they even use marijuana in 1894? What I hadn't expected was just another house, neatly nestled on one of the back streets catty-corner from the rear of the Mercantile Building.

Or, I realized as I followed him inside and got a good look around, a brothel. Or a bordello. Or a speakeasy. Or whatever they called them back then, given I wasn't sure of the difference between any of those words in the first place. A House of Ill Repute. Right in the middle of Conconully. Deserted at the moment, due to the circumstances I guessed, but otherwise the maze of little rooms looked like something out of that one bit in *Shanghai Noon*. Or maybe *Butch Cassidy and the Sundance Kid* again. Now I was expecting Jackie Chan or Paul Newman to come strolling down the hall.

"The tunnel's down here." Max pointed.

"How did Tracy get through that dinky hole on the other end – never mind," I said, because I was now talking to Max's back, and followed him down a narrow flight of stairs to a dirt-floored cellar. One end was lined with shelves filled with bottles. Enough liquor, I guessed, to get the whole town drunk. But not illegal, not like pot would have been back now.

Max gestured toward the other end. It was dark enough I was half feeling my way already. He reached for the lantern, and I gave it to him. "Watch." He struck a match, opened the back, and lit the lantern deftly.

The beam coming through that glass bull's-eye looked almost like a flashlight. I made to take the lantern from him, but Max wasn't done yet. He pushed at a little lever-like thing on its side, and metal slid across the inside of the bull's-eye, blocking the light. By the time he'd closed it all the way, you'd never have known the lantern was lit. He reopened it and grinned at me.

"Cool," I told him. And it was. Almost as good as a flashlight.

His eyebrows went up, but he only told me, "Hook it to your belt."

But not quite as good. I wasn't about to set my jeans on fire. "I can carry it."

He shrugged and handed it to me. "Suit yourself."

"Thanks." And I meant it, at least about the demonstration.

His eyes shone impatiently in the beam of light. "Well, what are you waiting for?"

I wondered about that myself. "You keep an eye on this end of the tunnel in case he gets past me," I told him.

Max pulled another antique pistol out of his holster. "Not through me, he won't."

I nodded. Then, lantern in one hand, Colt in the other, I plunged into the tunnel.

* * *

It was a helluva dark, dank place. Moisture beaded on packed earth walls I could have touched on both sides at the same time, and slicked the rocky, uneven ground beneath my boots. I didn't have to duck, not quite, except for the tree roots hanging down like claws trying to strafe my scalp. Every time one of them managed it, I wanted to shudder.

I wondered just how much dirt was over my head, and how well compacted it was, and what the chances were of it collapsing in on top of me, and if anyone would be able to pinpoint where I was buried well enough to dig me out before I suffocated to death.

Funny how a guy can forget all about facing down an outlaw with a gun when his totally irrational fear is shoved into his face. I had a nice case of claustrophobia going by the time I finally made it to where there were boards overhead instead of dirt. I should have been seeing the sunlight from the display window, if the trap door had been open like I'd expected.

But it was closed. I still should have been able to see the light around the edges, though. Or through the cracks between the boards. I could see the ladder by the light of my lantern, leaning on the wall just below where the door should be. But I couldn't even see the door's edges.

I stared up at the underside of the floor, then down at my full hands. I couldn't climb the ladder without dumping the gun or the lantern, and I needed both. Even if I'd had a holster I wouldn't have put the gun in it. I was no Sundance Kid, able to yank it out and fire in a split second. I wanted the Colt ready in my hand.

I closed the bull's-eye, leaving myself in utter darkness so I didn't give myself away. As I hooked the lantern to my belt by feel, all I could think was I sure hope I don't set myself on fire after all.

* * *

The ladder, thank God, took my weight with only a groan or two. I reached above my head and felt the boards, searching for the trap door.

Ha! An edge, so tightly fitted I'd almost missed it. I traced around it with my fingers, noting, without much surprise, that the door was bigger than it had looked from the top. Big enough to climb through, at least.

But what the hell was on the other side?

Only one way to find out. I pushed slowly, hoping it wouldn't make any noise. The whole thing came loose pretty easily, no hinges, no nothing, and I slid it to one side as quietly as I could.

The darkness above me was as absolute as it was in the tunnel. Pitch black. I resisted the urge to reach down for the lantern just yet, and cocked my head, listening with all my might.

Complete and utter silence. No voices, no footsteps, not even any creaks from the building. No breathing, except my own. I held my breath, the hair on the back of my neck standing on end from the creepiness of how total the silence was.

At least there was no way anyone could be in whatever the room above me was. I let my breath out in a whoosh and poked my head through the trap door, my eyes barely above the level of the floor.

I unhooked the lantern from my belt and slowly raised it through the door. Felt for the little lever, and slowly slid it over.

I didn't slide it much, just enough to see where I was.

Just enough to see the man sitting on a crate, his back propped against the wall. His gun was aimed directly at me.

CHAPTER 16

He didn't get up. He didn't say anything as he squinted at the light. His gun never wavered, but he didn't shoot. I must have blinded him with the lantern, was all I could think. The effect wouldn't last long.

I jerked the Colt up faster than I thought I'd have been able to. I stared down his gun barrel, and he stared down mine.

"Well, sheriff," he drawled at last, "looks like we got ourselves a standoff."

Damn if the man didn't even sound like some sort of stereotyped outlaw. He made me want to laugh, which was not a good thing under the circumstances. I didn't know how real his bullets were, but it wasn't as if I wanted to find out. "Oh, I don't think so. Drop your gun or I'll fire."

He laughed, but he didn't drop his gun, which didn't leave me with much of a choice. So I fired. The racket in the enclosed space about deafened me, and the recoil damned near knocked me off the ladder.

Harry Tracy, or at least I assumed that's who he was, dropped his gun and fell sideways off his chair. He stared at me while I stared at the hole in his arm. I'd actually hit him.

It was the first time I'd ever aimed at a man. I have to say it stunned me.

Until I saw the blood puddling underneath him. I scrambled up through the hole and threw open the door, which, to my astonishment, not that I was giving it much thought at the time, opened into the bay window display space. Hoping I'd be heard from there, I called out, "It's all right, you can come in now."

The front door flew open, then the door from the hall. Faces peered through.

"Somebody get me some rope. And somebody get Doc Amy. I've got a wounded man here."

"Yes, sir, Sheriff." A couple of them dashed off. Others stared openly at Harry Tracy, the first man I'd ever shot.

I hadn't shot to kill, but even after the lucky shot with the wolf I didn't trust my aim with the Colt. I was pretty sure it was just a flesh wound, and it *had* kept him from shooting me. But he just lay there. And he wouldn't stop bleeding.

What the hell was taking Amy so long? She should have been out there waiting, just in case. I folded my bandanna into a makeshift bandage and pressed it against the wound.

Tracy cried out.

"The doctor's coming," I told him.

"Don't want no damned doctor." His voice was a raspy whisper.

He was an idiot. "Don't be a coward. She'll patch you up, and then you can face the music. You're going to live, unlike that poor bastard you shot over in Molson, and you're going to do it so you can rot in prison.

"Speaking of which, you have the right to remain silent." I finished Mirandizing him as he stared at me.

"What the hell was that?"

"I don't want you getting out on a technicality."

"Tech–" His voice was getting weaker, I didn't know why. Shock, maybe.

"Don't you pass out on me." I looked up, but nobody was there. "Amy!" I bellowed. "Where are you?"

Tracy's eyes rolled up and his head lolled back. "Oh, shit." Now what was I supposed to do?

Gently I laid him back down on the wooden floor. Picked up his limp hand and put it on the pad on his other arm. Maybe the deadweight – bad choice of words – would hold it until I could drag Amy in here where she belonged.

I could see his chest moving, though, so he must be breathing. Shallow and fast. Definitely shock.

I got myself up and went out the front door, but everyone was gone. Where the hell were they?

It didn't matter. I'd read them the riot act later. I went searching for Amy.

* * *

She was at the Fogles', of all places. I was headed toward her little house on Chesaw Street when I heard her laughter spill out of the open window. I swear I'd recognize that sound anywhere. I stopped abruptly, then strode up to the front door and pounded on it.

I was about ready to pound on it a second time when it swung open. I barely managed to jerk my fist back before I clocked her. "What the hell are you doing here?"

Amy gave me a puzzled look, which changed to a frown as I watched. "If you really need to know, I'm tending a patient."

"What about Harry Tracy?"

"Who?"

Okay. This wasn't funny anymore. I grabbed her by the arm and yanked her out onto the porch. "Harry Tracy. The bandit? The Butch Cassidy wannabe? He'd bleeding to death in the Mercantile Building as we speak." I dragged her back to the open door. "Mrs. Fogle?"

Tim popped his head around the corner. "Ma's resting."

"Fine," I said. "Go get Doc Amy's bag, please." Tim looked at Amy, his face worried. "Now, Tim," I added.

He disappeared back around the corner.

"You're hurting me." She sounded more indignant than in pain, so I loosened my grip, but damned if I was going to let her go.

"I need to get back in there. Patsy Fogle has an infection."

"There's a man dying. She can wait till you've got him stabilized."

"Dying?"

What was it going to take to get through to her?

"Yeah. I shot him."

Her eyes went wide. "Shot who?"

"Harry Tracy. Amy, what's the matter with you?"

She opened her mouth, but just then Tim came dashing back with her black bag, and I grabbed it with my free hand. "Never mind. Come on."

"All right. But Dan, Harry Tracy's dead."

How would she know? "Not yet he isn't."

I could feel her eyes boring into the back of my head as I dragged her down the block toward the Mercantile, but she didn't say anything else. Our feet thumped the wooden boardwalk, the only sound in the silence except for the wind in the unfurling green maple leaves over our heads.

I dragged her into the storage room and came to a grinding halt.

"What the hell–" I dropped Amy's hand.

"Do you feel all right, Dan?" she asked, peering up into my face.

"No," I said decisively. I sagged against the doorframe, feeling almost as if I'd been shot myself.

Amy left my side and went back to the display window. The pig stood on the raised floor of the bay window, positioned as if it wanted to look out, to see the town going by.

But that wasn't the big deal. Harry Tracy's gunshot wound hadn't been fatal. I knew it hadn't been. But it had caused him to bleed a fair amount, and the last I'd seen of him, five minutes ago, he'd been passed out on the storage room floor.

But now the wooden floorboards were as clean and pale as if they'd been sawn and laid yesterday. Smooth, too. The trap door had vanished, as well. It took some effort, but I straightened, walked over and squatted down. Ran my hands over it.

I turned to stare up at Amy, visible through the doorway. "He must have been faking it." Faking all that blood? But there wasn't any other explanation. "He can't have gone far," I said. "Not bleeding like that. We've got to find him."

Amy came over and crouched beside me. "Who, Dan?"

Couldn't she hear me? "Harry Tracy."

"Didn't you hear me?" Her echo of my thoughts made me shiver. She put her hand on my shoulder. I didn't shake it off. It would have been petty. "Harry Tracy's dead," she continued, meeting my gaze straight on. "Shot in a holdup in Oroville a few weeks ago, or so we heard. And as much as I hate to say so, it was good riddance to bad rubbish. He terrorized the Okanogan country for years."

"Yeah," I said slowly. "So you told me." In so many words, as a matter of fact.

She patted my arm. "Why don't you come on back to the house? You look like you've had a hard day."

She stood and extended a hand to me. It was a good strong hand, one that had seen work and enjoyed it, the pulse beating lightly at her wrist.

I shook myself, and tried to remember why I was so confused. "Amy."

"Come on." She smiled down at me.

I grasped her hand, and hauled myself to my feet.

"And look!" she said when I was standing next to her. "You found the pig!"

I shrugged. "I didn't find it. It made its way back on its own, apparently." I followed her over to where the pig sat like the king of Conconully, surveying its domain.

She was petting it and crooning over it like it was some sort of live animal. "Oh, I've missed him. The town just wasn't the same without Harry."

She'd told me the thing's name before, but "Harry?" As in Harry Tracy?

"Tim named him."

"Oh."

"After a character in a book."

"Oh."

At last she glanced up. "Come on, let's go have a cup of tea."

I reached out and pulled her back to her feet again. "I thought you didn't do tea."

She laughed at me. I shook my head. She reached up and ran a hand down the side of my face, making it tingle. "Now that Harry's back, it's probably time we had a talk. And, as Audrey always says, a good talk requires a good cup of tea."

"Wait a minute." I squatted back down by the pig. I had to make sure.

"What are you looking for?" she asked, sounding amused.

"Just checking something." I ran my hand along the planks under the pig's four plaster feet. The boards were smooth here, too, for the most part. A bit wavy in spots, with a knot in the wood here and there. But there was no handle. No hole cut and then filled in with a trap door here, either. And I'd be willing to bet my badge there was no tunnel under either of those smooth wooden floors.

I stood. "Okay, let's go."

"Did you find what you were checking for?"

"No," I said lightly.

"It doesn't seem to be bothering you much."

"No." What was the point? Nothing in this town was what it seemed to be. Except what really mattered.

We let ourselves out of the Mercantile Building, and, after I pulled on the door to make sure it was locked, I reached out and took Amy's hand. She smiled up at me and laced her fingers through mine.

"Come on." We strolled down the spring-warm maple-shaded streets toward home.

Chapter 17

When we arrived there, however, Rob and Audrey were waiting for us. Amy didn't seem surprised, although I wished they'd go find something else to do. I didn't really care much for tea, but the kettle was already whistling as three of us sat down at the table. Audrey bustled about, setting out cherry pie from the hoard I'd received for wolf duty as well as sugar and milk and silverware.

"Sit down, Audrey," Rob said at last. "This isn't a party."

"Much you know," Audrey returned, but she did sit down, thank God. Then apparently she had to make the tea into a kind of ritual, sitting behind the brown china pot like some sort of domestic goddess. I glanced over at Amy and watched her watching Audrey with something that looked almost like envy.

I took a bite of pie. "Wait," said Rob.

I swallowed and set my fork down. "Oh, sorry."

Audrey handed the cups around. They were thin, fine china, and I hoped to hell I wouldn't drop or break mine.

"Do you care for milk?" she asked me.

I grimaced. "No. No, thanks." I was pretty sure there wasn't going to be much to make this stuff taste like anything but medicine.

"So," Rob said when everything was arranged to Audrey's satisfaction. He picked up his cup. Audrey and Amy followed suit, and after a second so did I.

He lifted his like he was raising a glass of champagne. So did Audrey and Amy. After a moment, feeling pretty stupid, so did I.

"To Conconully," Rob said, and sipped his tea.

"To Conconully," Audrey and Amy echoed, and sipped theirs.

They all looked at me. "To Conconully," I said resignedly. Amy kicked me under the table. My tea sloshed but didn't spill. I glared at her and took a drink.

It tasted like – tea. I'm not sure what I was expecting, but not just plain old Lipton. I started to drink some more, but Amy put her hand on my arm.

This time Audrey led the toast. "To home."

Rob and Amy, and me, this time, echoed her. "To home." With them, I took another drink.

The caffeine seemed to be kicking in faster than usual, given the amount in my system had to be measured in molecules.

Amy lifted her cup. "To belonging." She sipped from her cup. .

"To belonging," we echoed, and drank.

They set their cups down. I held mine up.

Amy cocked her head at me. "Did you have something to say, Danny?"

"Yeah." Much to my own surprise, I did.

"What is it?"

"Pick up your cups," I told the three of them. They did. Not without a certain amount of amusement, I could tell. Rob was outright grinning.

I could feel the heat rising in my face. Get this over with, Reilly, I thought. "To the people who took me in. Thanks."

Amy's free hand squeezed mine. "We're glad you're here," she said.

"That indeed we are," added Audrey.

We drank.

* * *

"So," I said after my last bite of cherry pie was gone, "Let me see if I've got this straight."

They all looked at me expectantly.

"I've wandered into some sort of alternate universe."

The other two just looked puzzled, but Amy laughed. "You could put it that way."

Audrey stood and began gathering up the tea things.

"You don't need me for this," Rob added. "And I've got work to do."

Amy waved Rob off. I turned my attention back to her as the front door closed behind him. "Well?"

"I don't think there is a way to explain this without sounding like we're all crazy," Amy said. "Audrey?"

Audrey looked over her shoulder from her place at the sink and smiled. "You're doing just fine."

"I haven't even started yet," Amy complained.

"If you can explain how that bandit went from bleeding out where I shot him to having died weeks ago somewhere else entirely, and where that pig went and how it came back, and why there's no electricity and no running water, and how come you've got no clue what a cell phone is, or even tell me what the hell day it is—"

"Mind your language, young man," Audrey said. Without looking over her shoulder at us this time.

Amy smirked. "She's right, you know. If you're going to stay here you need to learn how to fit in a bit better."

"The way you never have?" Audrey asked.

"Audrey." Amy sighed. "Make up your mind. Either you're going to be part of this conversation or you're not."

"Hmph," was Audrey's only answer.

I got up and went behind Amy to pull out her chair. "C'mon. Let's go for a walk."

"All right."

"Don't forget about the dance," Audrey said.

"Is that tonight?" I asked.

"Yes," Amy said. She grasped my hand and pulled me out through the door. Behind me, I could hear Audrey muttering something about young people having no sense of time.

I looked down at Amy, and she looked back at me. "Right, Audrey," she called back through the open window. "I don't think you can blame that on us."

* * *

We walked down the street in silence for a bit. I had already asked some of my questions, and I could tell she was trying to figure out where to start.

At last she said, "I don't know if I'd call it an alternate universe. More a place where time has pretty much stopped."

Granted, that's what it felt like, but – "Time doesn't stop, Amy."

"No, I suppose not." She swung my hand in hers, then asked, "What year was it when you came here?"

Startled, I said, "2014."

"Wow. Twenty-nine years. It doesn't seem that long."

"That long since when?"

"Since I came here."

I stared at her. "Just how old are you?"

She grinned. "Twenty-six."

162

"You came here before you were born?"

She was still grinning, her eyes mischievous. "No. I was twenty-five when I came here, and I added a year because I figured it had to be at least that long." She sobered. "People do eventually age and fade away here – I've seen it happen. But time doesn't move here the way it did in the real world. I'm not sure if a day here equals a year there or vice versa, or if there's any correlation at all. I'm probably not really twenty-six, but there's no way to calculate it, so age doesn't really mean much here."

I opened my mouth, then closed it again.

"As for Harry Tracy, I don't know how that works, either, really. I just know he shows up – look, let me just call it every year, I don't know what else to call it. I don't think he's real, or at least I don't think he's as real as we are. The wolf is the same, although it may be a real wolf that wanders in and gets caught in this place, because it seems a lot more random. And because we do have other critters."

"I've seen squirrels," I offered.

"Yes, and deer and mice and birds and everything else living in this part of the world. Even bears."

She glanced up at me, then away. "I'm the only one who sees the pattern, though. Or at least the only person who admits to it."

"Why did you play innocent with me, then?" I asked.

She gave me a sheepish look. "I'd forgotten what it was like, I guess. I think the reason I see the pattern is because I haven't been here as long as everyone else. I tried to talk to Rob about it once not long after I arrived here, but he just got up and walked away. I think he knows, though."

I finally managed to get the words out. "Knows what, Amy?"

She squeezed my hand. "That this place is different."

I snorted. "You can say that again."

"If you want to know why it's different, I can't tell you, because I don't know myself. I think I used to, back when I first came here, but I can't remember, and, honestly?" She stopped and, grasping my other hand, too, swung herself around to face me. "I don't care anymore. This is a good place, Dan. I don't want to go back to where I was. I think I was unhappy there." She sagged slightly, standing there in front of me. "But I can't stop you from leaving, even though I really don't want you to."

I didn't know what to say to that. When I'd first arrived here, I'd wanted nothing more than to go back. I'd thought this place was nuts. I still thought it, and everyone who lived here, was out of their collective tree. But as I looked around at the tidy street with its white-painted false front buildings, at the people striding purposefully or strolling aimlessly by, at that damned pig in the window of the Mercantile Building–

"Tell you what," I said to her, letting go of her hands and nudging her back to my side. "You explain that," I cleared my throat in lieu of a swearword, "pig, and maybe then I'll be able to give you an answer."

Her lips twitched, and she started forward again. "I'm not sure I'm going to be able to explain Harry to your satisfaction. All I can really tell you is that because he came back and you're still here, that's how we knew you might truly stay."

"So that chunk of plaster is some sort of fortune teller?"

"He's not just a chunk of plaster," Amy said indignantly, but she squeezed my hand again. "When I arrived here–" She took a breath. "When I arrived here, I was the first person since the beginning who decided to stay. They threw a party for me. And in the middle of the party, after he'd been missing for days, just like this time, Harry reappeared, like some kind of good omen, and, well, it was sort of the icing on the cake, because I don't think anyone here believed I'd really stay until he returned."

"Which is why you were so dam– so glad when it showed back up today."

"Yes."

I had to ask. "Amy, how did you come to arrive here? Not what happened right after you got here, but how did you get here? You said something about an accident. Did you wreck your car, too?"

She frowned. "I don't really remember anymore."

That scared me a bit, although I wasn't sure why. "Will I forget, too? After a while?"

"I don't know." Her voice was earnest when she added, "Does it matter?"

I thought about it long enough for us to make it clear out past the edge of town. The air was getting chilly.

"We need to turn around now," Amy said.

I didn't argue with her, but swung around and headed back.

"Does it?" she asked.

I took a deep breath and let it out. "I don't know."

She nodded understanding, but she wouldn't meet my gaze.

I stopped, almost to the first house at the edge of town. "Amy? What about the tea?"

Now she looked amused. At my expense. "It's just tea."

I believed that about as far as I could throw her. Well, I probably could have thrown her at least a yard or two, she was so tiny, but never mind. "No, it's not. Or you wouldn't have made such a big deal about it the first time Audrey offered me a cup."

"She was pushing you too fast. She wanted you to stay, after all the trouble we went through to bring you here–"

"Amy," I said gently. "I'm not stupid. And I do still remember. Where did she get the truck? And how did she manage to leave town?"

"The truck wasn't the hard part. Rob likes to tinker with mechanical stuff. He's the one who got it running."

"Where did you get it in the first place?"

"You'd have to ask Max. He's the one who found it originally. Before my time."

"And?" I added.

"I don't *know*," she said, finally exasperated with me. Maybe frustrated, too. "Honestly, I don't. The first I knew of what was happening they were carrying you into town on a pallet with a bump on your head and a broken hand." She took a deep breath. "I don't know how they did it. I didn't know they could. I'm sorry."

I shrugged. "Not much you could have done." I let it go after that, mostly because I had too much churning around in my brain to keep any kind of a conversation going, all the way to her house on the other end of town.

When we reached her doorstep she turned to look up at me and took both my hands. "I am so glad you're here, Danny. You do know that, right?"

"Yeah." I let go of her hands, but only so I could wrap my arms around her and tuck her head under my chin. It wasn't her fault. I did believe that. Whatever the town had done to bring me here, it wasn't her fault.

"What time should I pick you up for this shindig?"

She leaned back to look at me and smiled, but it didn't reach all the way to her eyes. "We don't have to go if you don't want to."

"You don't think they'd come after us?"

"Not if I asked them not to." She paused. "They meant well, Danny. They had their reasons. And I don't think you'd be here if you'd been happy in the real world."

I thought about that. Thought about Mom's leaving when I was eight and never coming back. About Dad and Carol and their new family and how I never had fit in. About the patrol academy and thinking I'd finally found my place in the world, only to be sent out here to the back of beyond where I didn't know anybody. And about Linda.

I gazed down at Amy, who seemed sincere when she said she wanted me to stay. I wouldn't have to worry about her being dissatisfied with where life took me.

Yeah, mostly because if I decided to stay, I'd never be able to leave. Funny how it didn't seem like such a bad deal. I wondered if I would change my mind down the road. Probably not.

This really wasn't her fault. I smiled down at her. "Is seven too early?"

She beamed back at me. "Make it seven-thirty. I need time to primp enough to make Belinda happy."

"All right. I'll pick you up then."

"I'm looking forward to it."

Funny, so was I. Reluctantly, I let her go. When she glanced back as she closed the door, her eyes were smiling, too.

Chapter 18

I wasn't surprised at all to find another, dressier, new suit of clothes spread across my bed when I got back. And, of course, when I put them on, they fit me perfectly. Belinda really was a wizard with a needle, and I told her so when she stopped by just after supper to check on her handiwork.

"Go on with you," was all she said, but she had me stand in the middle of my room like a department store dummy while she ran her hand across the shoulders of my new jacket, and knelt down to tug at the hem of my new trousers. Even the boots were new, and I did wonder how she managed that, but knew better than to ask.

At last she was satisfied, and let me go. I couldn't help but feel like I was heading off to the prom I'd never attended properly.

"You'll be stopping by Cassandra's for flowers, of course," Belinda said, brushing nonexistent dust off the front of my suit coat.

"I guess so." Yup. Just like a prom. "Um, where's Cassandra's?"

"Back on Oroville Street, behind the Mercantile. Little white house with green shutters."

Uh-huh, I thought. I raised my eyebrows.

She nodded. "You know where I mean."

"Yeah." From brothel to flower shop in what? Twenty-four hours? Except it probably hadn't been twenty-four hours in their minds, and I wasn't sure it was in mine anymore, either.

"Get on with you, then. You don't want to be late."

Curious, I asked, "Will you be there?"

She smiled. I think it was the first time I'd ever seen her smile. "I wouldn't miss it."

"Well," I told her, grinning, "you'd better get a move on, too."

She looked down at herself, in what I now knew was just an everyday sort of floor-length skirt and blouse. "I suppose I should."

I waved a hand at her as I left. "See you there."

* * *

Cassandra's wasn't a regular florist, obviously. The front room of the former brothel was full of bouquets and bunches of flowers obviously picked from someone's garden, sitting on every flat surface the room afforded. Much nicer than a regular florist.

Cassandra herself was someone I hadn't met yet, a small, brown-haired woman with green eyes and a rabbit-like expression that opened up cheerfully when I couldn't help but gaze around in pleasure.

Call me a wimp, but I like flowers. I like the colors and the smells and everything about them. And garden bouquets like these reminded me of my mother. In a good way. Of digging in the dirt while she worked in her garden when I was little, of picking flowers I knew I wasn't supposed to and taking them to her, only to have her laugh and hug me. From before the day I came home from school and she was gone. Not that it was anyone's business but my own.

Still. I walked around and sniffed and looked and touched, trying to look like I was having a hard time making up my mind, so as to disguise the fact that I was enjoying myself.

After a bit, Cassandra said, "These are Amy's favorites," pointing to a pretty little handful of blue bachelor's buttons and yellow roses. The roses had a scent that wafted up into my back brain the way Amy's scent did.

"Well, then," I said, "I guess I'll take those."

Payment didn't seem to be an issue. "Will you be at the dance tonight?" I asked.

She smiled and ducked her head. "Yes. Everyone will be there tonight."

"You save a dance for me, then," I told her.

"Thank you."

Once I was outside, I looked around furtively, but I guess most people were home getting ready for the party, because I didn't see anyone. I couldn't resist. I stuck my nose in one of those gorgeous yellow roses and took a big sniff, then headed on my way.

* * *

When I reached Amy's little cottage on the edge of town, I discovered my hands were sweaty enough that the stems of the bouquet were damp. I loosened my grip on them slightly, and knocked.

The vision who opened the door was something to behold. Royal blue satin trimmed with white lace fit like a glove from her breasts to her hips, then swept to the floor, and pale blonde hair caught back from her face shone down her back like a river of ice. Her eyes were midnight dark against her pale skin. All that pale skin, and curves I hadn't realized she had... You could have warned me you were going to show her off like that, Belinda, I thought. Or maybe it was just as well she hadn't. "Wow," I said when I got my voice back, "you clean up great."

She snickered, and became Amy again. "So do you."

"Thanks. I feel like I'm going to a costume party."

"I always feel like I'm at a costume party here."

I laughed. "You've got a point. Well, let's do this right." I held out the bouquet. "These are for you."

Her eyes gleamed in amusement. "They're lovely."

"They look good with your dress, too."

"Sometimes it's nice to be girly." There was an odd note in her voice I couldn't quite place, but she shook herself. "We'd better get going. We don't want to be late."

"You're the third person to say that to me in the last hour or so," I told her. "I didn't think time was that big a deal here."

"Oh, it isn't. But you don't want to miss any of the fun, do you?"

I wanted to roll my eyes, but, oddly enough, no, I didn't want to miss any of it. Whatever that fun turned out to be. "Of course not." I held out my arm. She took it.

Yup. I definitely felt like I was heading to the prom. At least I wasn't going to have to try to load that dress on a motorcycle.

* * *

The closer we got to the Mercantile Building, the more people we saw. Everyone was dressed up to one degree or another, obviously the best clothes each person had. I even saw top hats and tail coats on some of the men, and blessed Belinda for not trying to put an outfit like that on me. The women wore every shade of the rainbow in silk and shine, and Cassandra must have disposed of her entire stock of flowers among them. Even the kids, more of them than I remembered seeing since I'd arrived here, were in what was obviously their Sunday best.

The street was full of chatter and laughter as we approached the front doors of the Mercantile. They were thrown wide open, light from every gas jet in the place blazing out into the starlit night. Max, one of those top hats adding almost a foot to his lack of height and a tail coat brushing the backs of his knees, stood by the doorway, welcoming each group inside with beaming handshakes and bows.

When he saw me, his smile became a smirk. "Glad you could make it, Sheriff Reilly. Doc Amy."

"Behave, Max," Amy said. "Don't ruin the evening."

"I wouldn't dream of it," Max said, and waved us on through.

"What was that all about?" I murmured in her ear, taking a whiff of the scent of her, which really was like the roses.

"Just Max being Max, as usual. He's always got to know more than everyone else." She drew away slightly. "You need to behave, too, you know."

"I always behave," I began indignantly, then we stepped into the ballroom, and I closed my mouth abruptly.

Yeah, it was the same enormous barn-like place we'd decorated with crepe paper streamers and Japanese lanterns three? or was it four? days ago, but it couldn't have been more different if it had tried.

CHAPTER 19

I'd never have recognized it if I hadn't known what it was. It looked like the masquerade party scene from that old movie of Cinderella my stepmother used to watch all the time, the one with Drew Barrymore, except no one was wearing a mask. Or like the ballroom in *Titanic*. I knew it was all an illusion, that in reality it wasn't any fancier than a dressed-up high school gym. But you couldn't have proved it by me just then.

"So," I asked Amy, "does it all turn into a pumpkin at midnight?"

"Not exactly." She winked at me. She started to say something else, but closed her mouth as the music began and people started swirling by like they'd been taught by Fred Astaire himself.

This wasn't anybody's high school prom.

I was more than content to watch, well, stare with my mouth hanging open, until Amy reached up and tapped me on the shoulder. "Pretty spectacular, isn't it?"

"I'd never have believed it, not in a million years."

"That's how I felt the first time, too."

"They do this regularly?"

"Yes. Aren't you going to ask me to dance?"

"Um, Amy, I don't know how to dance like that."

"Sure you do." She took my hand and put it around her waist, then grasped my other hand with hers and pulled me out into the crowd.

And, no, I didn't know how to dance like that. I still don't know how to dance like that. I still can't figure out how I managed not to make an absolute idiot out of myself, but by the time that piece of music ended, I was waltzing. Sort of. One-two-three, one-two-three. I can still feel the rhythm when I think about that night.

The music came from the little bower Amy had draped with crepe paper the day we'd decorated the place. Two violins, a cello, and a piano, played by three grizzled old miners and the crazy little old lady from the tree, of all people, with way more skill than I'd have guessed from their looks. They played one tune after another, none of which I recognized, but then why would I? Not always waltzes. It was just the only rhythm which sounded even vaguely familiar. People bobbed and wove through some sort of peculiar line dance where they faced each other, and they swung around arm in arm, and they did all kinds of steps I'd never seen people do at dances before.

I got dragged in, not just by Amy, but by Cassandra, who reminded me I'd promised her a dance and by Patsy Fogle, who seemed to be feeling much better, and even by Audrey, who told me, and I quote, "Now that you've done this a few times, I think I can trust you not to step on my toes." And by half a dozen others. But not by Belinda, whom I spotted sitting with a bunch of older ladies watching the rest of us look ridiculous instead of getting out there and being ridiculous themselves.

I'd never, in all my life, seen anything like it, and I wouldn't have missed it for the world.

Max would have been breaking fire codes all over the place if there'd been any to break. I had no idea how many people crowded the room, but it was more than I'd realized existed here. And still they came, and still they danced, and still they ate and talked and laughed.

I caught a glimpse of little Betsy Fogle, who sat wide-eyed under the piano, and of Tim and a bunch of his buddies knotted together in a corner, watching a giggling bunch of girls watching them.

"Come on," I said to Amy, and headed over toward the boys.

"What? Why?" she said, but she went along with me.

"Hey, Tim," I called as we got closer.

The boy looked up at me, startled at first, but then relaxing as he recognized me.

"Hey, Sheriff."

"Why aren't you out there?" I asked him, just to get his reaction.

"With *girls?*" He sounded like, well, like a ten-year-old boy.

"Yeah. That redhead's been eyeing you for about half an hour now." I'd have been willing to bet good money on it, anyway, judging from the way she blushed when she noticed Tim looking at her.

"Missy Brown?" His voice cracked.

What could I bribe him with? I didn't have anything here— Inspiration struck. "If you dance with her, come by my office Monday and I'll let you hold my gun." I needed to turn one room of my house into an office, didn't I?

Amy drew her breath in and opened her mouth. I added before she could object, "Unloaded, of course."

"Really?" His eyes were wide.

I couldn't help grinning. "Yeah, really. Is that worth it to you?"

Tim gave me a nod worthy of a knight going into battle. It would have been a lot more effective if he hadn't looked so terrified.

I turned to the other boys. "Same goes. You dance at least one dance with a girl, you can come along and hold it, too."

Without waiting to see what happened, I led Amy back out onto the floor.

"You monster," she said, laughing. "What on earth possessed you?"

"The girls will enjoy it, won't they?"

"It will make their entire evening," she said with conviction as I mentally counted one-two-three and tried not to let the kids notice I was watching them.

"How many do you count?"

Amy laughed. "Every last mother's son of them."

I shrugged. "If I can do it, they can do it."

"Misery loves company?" We swung past one of the boys, a determined look on his face as he stared at their feet, and the beaming little girl he was – well, marching might be a better description than dancing – around the room. As I watched, he glanced up at her, and his face turned bright red.

"Ah, puppy love," Amy said, and squeezed the hand she held.

I met her eyes.

She sighed, and we began to make our way to the edge of the room. We reached the stage, and I lifted her to sit on it, then rested an elbow next to her.

"From your face," Amy said. "I'm thinking your personal pumpkin may have arrived."

I hesitated. "Not exactly."

"Then what is it?"

I really didn't want the answer, but I had to ask. "Will those children ever grow up?"

"Of course." But her voice was too quick and bright.

"Really?"

She stared down at her blue satin lap. I reached out and put a finger under her chin, lifting it so she had to look at me. "How much older has Tim gotten in the last twenty-five years?"

"It hasn't been twenty-five years here."

"You said people fade away. That's not the same thing as dying."

She gave me a sharp glance. "It might as well be. They're missed just as much, and they're just as gone."

"How do you feel about staying twenty-six years old forever?"

"I won't. Max promised—" she shut her mouth abruptly.

"What did Max promise, Amy?"

She shook her head at me.

"Hey, this is supposed to be a happy occasion," said the man himself from behind me.

"Sorry, Max," Amy said and jumped down, her skirt billowing around her. "I believe I owe you a dance."

Max looked inquiringly at me. "Do you mind, Sheriff?"

I wondered what he'd say if I told him I did. "Go on."

"I'll come find you after," Amy promised.

"Fine."

"Cassandra's looking kind of lonely," she added, pointing. "Why don't you go ask her—"

"Go on, Amy," I said, waving them off.

Max took her arm. "Yes, come, dear. The music is starting."

She went with him, but she turned her head to look back at me. I met her glance, and she turned away again.

Chapter 20

I leaned against the edge of the stage and watched the dancers for a bit, but the sheen had gone off for me. I'm still not sure why. It wasn't like I could do anything about those kids. Or about any of them. Or if they'd want me to, even if I could.

They had a life here. So did I. More of a life than I'd ever had back in the real world. So what if this place and these people were so far out in left field they couldn't see home plate? They appeared to be content.

Maybe they just didn't know better. Or know anything. Nobody seemed to be willing to tell me anything that made any sense. Or able to, for whatever reason.

I watched Max glide Amy around the room, her bright blue dress easy to pick out even in this crowd, even at her height. And his. They looked oddly suited to one another, actually. Not that I thought Max was romantically interested in her, or vice versa. More like father and daughter. Which suddenly bothered me more than the other would have.

Before I knew it, I was striding through the crowd of dancers right up to the two of them, and tapping Max on the shoulder. One-two – he stopped. "Cutting in, my boy?" he asked.

"Yes," I said. I glanced over at Amy, who was watching us both warily. "Is that all right with you?"

She didn't answer. Why did I have the impression she was uneasy about answering? That made no sense.

"It's up to you, you know." Max told Amy. His voice was smooth, and he was smiling, but the expression didn't reach his eyes.

She hesitated, then said, "If you don't mind, Max, then yes, it's all right."

Max dropped his hands, letting go of Amy's. Amy stepped back and let hers drop as well.

"It's your choice, girl," Max said. "I never meant it to be otherwise."

Amy smiled at the arrogant little man. "I know. Thanks for seeing it my way."

"Of course." He left us and began picking his way through the crowd.

I took her hand, but instead of taking up where Max left off, I headed across the broad expanse, toward the front of the ballroom.

"Wait." Amy held back.

"What?" I stopped and looked at her. "I need some air."

"I know. I do, too. But this is much closer." She pulled me toward the stage and around the side to the back door.

Feeling grateful out of all proportion to the solution, I shoved at it, and it creaked open like nobody'd been through it in years. "Must be the damp night air making it stick," I said as we stepped outside into the cool quiet.

"Ah," said Amy, and took a deep breath.

"Yeah." I let mine out. I felt like I'd been holding it for hours.

She smiled at me. "I think I've had enough party to last me a while."

No kidding. "Reading my mind?"

"No. Just honest." She took my arm. "Wait a minute."

When I did, she reached down with her free hand and lifted first one foot, then the other, to slip her shoes off. "Oh, that feels good." She wiggled her toes in the thick green grass.

I shook my head to dispel just how much I wanted to pick her up and carry her away. "What is it about women and shoes?"

"Oh, quit it. I skip the boots once. *Once.* And you have to make fun of me." She hooked the heels over her fingers and stretched her arms up. "Mmm. A night like this makes me feel as if I could live forever."

I considered that with more seriousness than I think she wanted me to. "I thought that was the point of this place."

"No, that's just a side benefit. Besides, it doesn't feel like forever."

I hadn't thought of it that way. "What does it feel like, Amy?"

"Being happy, and useful. As if I fit in."

I had to agree with her there. I didn't want to think what that said about me, so I changed the subject, surprising myself with the old-fashioned way I did it. "May I walk you home?"

Amy shook her head. "Not quite yet."

And, sure enough, as if on cue, Audrey stuck her head out the back door and said, "It's time."

Time for what?

Amy stepped back into her shoes, took my hand, and pulled me toward the door. "As soon as this part is done, Danny, I would be happy to have you walk me home."

The last thing I wanted to do was go back in there with the crowd and the noise, but it was obvious Amy wasn't giving me a choice. I took a deep breath of the cool night air, and thought, it's not for long.

As I followed Amy inside, I realized something was terribly wrong.

The ballroom had gone utterly silent. Oh, people were still standing cheek by jowl, smiling and gesturing, but they were still. Utterly motionless. I couldn't, I realized in shock, even hear them breathing, the way I hadn't been able to hear Harry Tracy breathe when I was in the tunnel.

"Amy, I've got to get out of here." I whispered the words, but I might as well have shouted them. No heads turned. Nobody answered me. Not even Amy. I tried to pull my hand out of hers, but she'd gone as stiff and motionless as the rest of them, her fingers clenched around mine like they were frozen there.

Like an iron filing to a magnet, my head swung around to stare at the stage, less than three feet away. Max stood on it, his feet planted as if they'd grown roots, next to that innocent-looking plaster pig. His hand rested on it as if casually, and as I watched, his fingers curled in almost a sort of caress.

He wasn't still. His eyes swept the frozen crowd. He looked almost comforted or relieved, as if he'd averted something terrible. Until his gaze met mine; then once more he transformed into the genial, arrogant Max I thought I'd known. I could feel myself shiver, even in the heat of the ballroom.

"It's all right, you know," he said in a conversational tone.

"Like fun it is." I was still whispering. I'm not sure why.

"They're all right. I'm not hurting them. They won't even remember."

"You've got them in some kind of a trance. Is this how you stop time?"

His expression changed again then. You know those photos of President Lincoln, the ones where he looks like he's lost his last friend?

I'd never seen an expression like that on a living person's face before. "I can't stop time," Max said. "If I could, I'd have done it– Well. No. But this is where you need to decide if you want to stay, Daniel Benjamin Reilly."

"But–"

"You thought you had?" He shook his head. "No, no. The tea, as Amy told you, is just tea." He stroked the statue's head, but I noticed he never broke contact with it. "Harry here is just a pig, although he's not made of plaster, in spite of what he looks like. Oscar and I found him. In the mine, the day before the flood. The day Oscar died and Rose lost her wits."

"Rose?" I couldn't help asking.

"Oscar's wife. Your friend in the tree." He sighed. "Things have never been the same for any of us since, and no, I don't know why. I wish I did." His gaze became intense. It was as if we were the only two people in the room. Or the world. He took a deep breath, and let it out. "However, I have discovered that unless we welcome newcomers, and make them our own, Conconully, like any other community, will cease to exist. I believe with all my heart that this would be a tragedy." He paused, then added, "I have tried to choose those who were unhappy enough in the wide world that they would not miss it if they never saw it again. Was I mistaken with you, Daniel? If so, I do deeply apologize."

No, he was dead on the money with my feelings about the world I'd left behind when I'd wrecked my cruiser. I didn't miss a damned thing about it. But how did he know? And telling him he was right? Admitting it? I couldn't do that, at least not out loud. "I take it you made a mistake with Miss Clancy? The schoolteacher?"

"Yes. Which is why Amy needed to choose. Why you need to choose, as well. I am sorry I tried to keep you in the dark as long as I did. You're smarter than I expected you to be, and you need to know what you're choosing."

Big of him, I thought. Then I looked at him. Really looked at him and realized what this was costing him. No one should have that much responsibility, I thought, and wondered if that was what had killed the hapless Oscar and made that sweet little old lady lose her wits.

It took a lot of will, but I closed my eyes and turned my head. When I opened them, I looked around the room. There was little Betsy Fogle, under the piano with some other children. And her brother Tim, still next to the little redheaded girl – Missy? And Rob, his arm around Audrey. And Belinda, in the corner with her cronies. And all the others. I glanced down at Amy and wished she'd let go of my hand, so I could put my arms around her and hold her and protect her from whatever the hell this was.

At last, at long last, I drew a deep breath and looked back up at Max. He was still standing there, still stroking that damned pig, a wistful smile playing around his mouth.

"Who the hell are you, Max?"

"I'm the person who keeps this town alive." I don't know what he saw in my face then. It made him sigh hard enough that I thought I saw the streamers sway from his breath, ten feet away. "Tomorrow," he added before I could get my mouth open to ask him how or why or why him or anything else, "is May 27th. Does that date mean anything to you?"

"No. But it can't be May 27th. It was November when I arrived here, and I've barely been here a couple of weeks. No way have I been here six months."

"You may have noticed, young man, that time is not the same here as it is in other places."

I snorted. "Yeah." And thought of Harry Tracy. "Neither are people's memories."

His fingers caressed the pig again. "That is necessary, and not something I can control even if I would," he told me. "I'm sure you can understand why."

Being stuck in a time warp and knowing you were stuck in a time warp were two different things, I had to admit. I nodded abruptly, wondering how it would feel to forget I'd shot a man. That I would shoot a man. Would I? Over and over? "Will I forget?"

Max shook his head. "I don't have that answer for you. But you've already altered the pattern, for what that's worth." He added abruptly, "You saved lives."

Then he changed the subject again before I could say anything. "If, after you walk Doctor Duvall home like a polite young gentleman and bid her good-night at her door with a kiss and nothing more" – his eyes glinted as if he knew I'd had other plans for the night, and suddenly I felt like I was back in Linda's folks' living room, her dad glaring at me while I waited for her to come downstairs – "and you continue on your way out Chesaw Street past the edge of town, you will come upon a historical marker. It's one you've seen before, I think. Read it again. Then go back to your comfortable home and climb into your comfortable bed. And think about what you want." He paused, then, as if it took him a great deal of effort, said, "By morning you will have chosen. Obviously, I hope you will stay with us. But if you don't, it *is* your choice." He paused again. "It was always your choice, Daniel. I do regret if at any point you've felt otherwise."

Before I could say anything back to him. Or before I could even get my fingers free from Amy's so I could go after him, he lifted his hand from that 'just a pig' and the room came alive again. Music and laughter and voices. Movement and smiles and dancing.

Amy squeezed my hand. "Are you ready to go?"

"Do you know what just happened?" I asked her.

Her smile faltered. "I didn't experience it, no. But I remember." She straightened. "I want one more dance before we go, Danny. Please?"

So we one-two-three-one-two-three'd across the ballroom along with the laughing crowd. I made sure to aim us toward the big wide front doors, and as the music ended, I put an arm around her and maneuvered us through the mob milling there.

We stepped out into the starlight. It took us longer than I'd have liked to get off the porch and down onto the street, what with all the good nights and all, but at last we were on our way down Okanogan Avenue.

"It was a great party, wasn't it?" Amy asked, swinging our hands.

"It was something," I agreed dryly.

She sobered. "That's not what I meant."

"It's kind of hard for me to think about anything else right now." Which pissed me off. I'd been looking forward to after the dance as much as I'd been looking forward to the dance, and now Max had found a way to mess that up, too. We turned down Chesaw Street and made our way to Amy's little house.

She let go of my hand. "Would you like to come in?"

I sighed. "I'd like to a whole lot."

"But?" She acted innocent about it, but I knew she knew.

I didn't have to do what Max told me. Like he'd said, it was my choice. Even if he hadn't told me so, I knew it was. But I needed to see that marker, damn him, and he knew I would. "I have something I need to do first. Would I still be welcome if I came back in a little bit and knocked on your door?"

"Of course." At least she had the grace to look disappointed.

"Thanks. Still..." I put my hands on her face, tilting it up toward mine. Bent down. And kissed her.

It got way more desperate way faster than I wanted it to. She was so soft, and so warm, and so real. And so alive. She had to be alive. A vision of her standing so still in that ballroom while Max and I had our idiotic discussion flashed through my brain and I held on too tightly. Deepened the kiss too fast. Too hard.

It took me a few seconds to realize she was trying to pull away. And more precious seconds to force myself to let go. "Hell. Are you all right?"

It was obvious she wasn't. Her face bore indentations from my fingers, and her eyes were shining, not in a good way, but from unshed tears.

"Oh, God. I'm sorry."

"No. No. Just let me catch my breath." After a moment, she said, "Are you sure you don't want to come in now and do whatever it is later?"

She still wanted me after that performance? Then it dawned on me. I could almost hear Max's words ringing in my brain. *I have discovered that unless we welcome newcomers, and make them our own, Conconully, like any other community, will cease to exist. I believe with all my heart that this would be a tragedy.*

Damn Max for making me doubt her. And myself. "No. It won't take long."

"Well, then, go on. I'll be here." Was that relief? It wasn't like I could ask.

I nodded, and waited till she went inside and the door closed behind her, then headed in the exact opposite direction to the way I wanted to go.

CHAPTER 21

Chesaw Street was longer than I'd realized it would be. Amy's was the last house before the woods took over, and soon the road turned into a bare track, heading upstream around a bend through the neck of the valley. The crick chimed over rocks and gravel. I strode along, the mash-up I felt, of frustration and anger and confusion, losing the battle with the peace and quiet of the place whether I wanted it to or not. By the time I reached my destination, I wasn't even breathing hard anymore.

The historical marker, sitting at the edge of a grassy meadow where the valley widened out again, hung from a crossbar suspended between a pair of uprights. All three were made of logs about six inches thick. The sign itself was made of planks fastened together horizontally, and the letters, painted white, were incised into the wood, which was painted dark brown. The effect, backdropped by the deep dark of the woods, made it look as if the shining letters were projected onto the air like a hologram, far brighter than they should have been, even given the full moon. Somehow this didn't surprise me in the least. "Okanogan County Historical Society" was carved into the crossbar, then, at the top of the sign itself, "The Conconully Story," and the text. I read slowly.

"Conconully sprang alive in 1886, as a riproaring mining camp known as Salmon City. The name changed to Conconully when the county seat came here in 1889. On May 27th, 1894, heavy rains in the watershed of Salmon Creek caused a runoff flood, which roared down the north fork of that stream, wiping out the entire town and killing 157 people. The reservoir on Salmon Creek above the old townsite, built in the early 1900s, was one of the first federal reclamation projects in the U.S. Conconully served as Okanogan County Seat from 1889 to 1894. It is believed that the Indians called this entire area, including the lake, Conconully, and in Indian it means 'the beautiful land of the bunch grass flats.' "

May 27th, 1894. Max had said tomorrow was May 27th. I sank down on a rock, a whole shitload of stuff clicking into place in my mind. I'd known they were stuck in the past. That was obvious. So now I had a date, and an event, that explained the way people here talked, the way they acted. The clothes they wore. No electricity. No phones. No rabies shots, or any other medicine that – well, no, that wasn't true. So when the hell had Amy ended up here? She knew phones, but not cell phones. She'd said she was an EMT, not a doctor, and she wore trousers when she could get away with it. And she'd thought 1894 was ninety years ago, not a hundred and twenty. She'd been here twenty-nine years, she'd said. Twenty-nine years in the outside world, at any rate, but not twenty-nine years here.

She'd said her arrival was an accident. Like my accident, maybe? Except, I thought suddenly, I hadn't had an accident. I'd been brought here. So had she, whether she wanted to believe it or not.

I took a deep breath. And another. And another. If all these people were ghosts, did that mean Amy and I were ghosts, too? I didn't feel like one. I felt real and solid. I remembered kissing Amy, just a little while ago. She'd felt about as real as real could get.

God, I was hungry. All of a sudden. I got up and nearly stumbled over a rock. Remembered the last time I'd gone too far out of town.

Where the hell was I? In a Stephen King novel? I needed to get back. Now. At least this time I wasn't freezing cold and dying of hypothermia.

I laughed. Right. Dying wasn't a possibility here. Well, yes, it was. Miss Clancy the schoolteacher had died, at least according to Max. I wondered if she'd not been unhappy enough in the real world, or if she'd changed her mind later. Or if she'd died on another May 26th when Max had explained all. But Max said I still had a choice. He couldn't have meant stay or die. That wasn't a choice.

I stumbled on, picking up strength as I went. I didn't want to think from where. I came around the bend in the valley, to see Conconully spread out before me. It was late. Most of the lights were out. A few last dancegoers straggled home.

For a moment, just a moment, I could see the silvery piles of lumber, bits of broken glass shining in the starlight, grass knee-high down the middle of the street. Then it snapped back, with a pop almost like a rubber band, and the town was there again, clean and shiny with smoke rising from stovepipes and chimneys, and whole windows reflecting the night.

I shook my head, wondered if Amy would be mad at me if I didn't show up back at her house, and passed it by, anyway. Her lamp was out. She'd probably given up on me and gone to sleep. The first raindrops splashed the dust just as I got home. Right on cue.

* * *

I startled awake to the crack of thunder at dawn the next morning, in spite of my late night. Rain clattered against my bedroom window, and lightning flashed against the steel gray sky as I sat up and rubbed my eyes. Another boom a few seconds later made me jump.

Rain's not a novelty to me – I grew up in Seattle, after all. But this was the first time I'd seen rain since I'd arrived in Conconully, and I hadn't realized how much I'd missed it. We don't get a lot of lightning and thunder west of the mountains, either. I watched the whole show with a grin on my face as I got up and dressed.

Then it hit me. Rain. For the first time since I'd arrived here, how long ago? The anniversary of the flood. My brain rebelled against the very idea, but it was what Max had been warning me about, in that oblique way of his. Max was going to make it flood, right on schedule. But even he couldn't do that. I thought about what he'd done last night, and – no. Just no.

When I arrived in the kitchen Audrey was there, of course, and so was my breakfast. I stopped halfway into the room, looking at her.

She'd looked elegant the night before, in a striped brown silk dress that rustled when she moved. This morning she looked no less elegant, but more strict, somehow. Not a party.

She frowned. "That's not what you want to wear to church," she told me. "The clothes you had on last night will do better."

"Church?" It was the last thing I'd been thinking of.

She frowned at me. "You're as bad as Doctor Amy was when she first arrived here. Doesn't anyone teach the Good Book anymore?"

"Yes, they do." Not that I still believed. My parents hadn't been into religion when I was little. When I'd asked my mother about it, she'd said she preferred to worship out in the wonder of nature, and we'd always spent our Sundays outdoors, in the garden, in the mountains, on an occasional trip to the beach. When she left, and my dad remarried, my stepmother had been more into organized religion, but by then it really hadn't taken. I hadn't been to church since I'd left for the academy.

But it didn't mean I didn't know my Bible. Carol had made sure of that. "My stepmother took us to church every Sunday."

"Well. I'm glad to hear that."

"I'd just forgotten it was Sunday." I hadn't thought days of the week – or the month, or the year – mattered here. But they did now.

She smiled at me. "Eat up, then, and go get dressed."

"Yes, ma'am."

I ate. The food was as delicious as ever, but somehow it felt like something was missing. Like eating cotton candy, taking a mouthful and having it melt away before I could swallow it.

I finished it, anyway, and went to change clothes. My suit could have been more wrinkled than it was, I'm sure, but I smoothed the fabric out as best I could, and made myself as presentable as possible.

Made my ablutions in the water from the pitcher and basin. Slicked my hair back.

Wondered if I should go pick up Amy, or if she'd want to have anything to do with me since I hadn't come back last night.

Decided to do it, anyway.

Walked out the front door of my house, looked up Okanogan Avenue toward Chesaw Street, and saw Salmon Creek.

Now, normally, the creek was just a little trickle of water ambling along the extension of Chesaw Street, around the hill through the valley just outside town, and down one side of Okanogan Avenue. Not even enough water to need a bridge, just a set of stepping stones every few yards.

The stepping stones were gone, hidden under a steady stream bouncing and frothing, filling the creekbed. As I watched, the water rose perceptibly.

The rain had slacked off, was just dripping from the trees more than falling from the sky by then. Another bolt of lightning sparked in the distance, and another crack of thunder rolled and echoed through the mountains surrounding the town. And, in a few moments, another. And another.

As I watched, ladies lifted their skirts to keep them from getting soaked, and men lifted children over the stream on their way to the church whose bell was pealing out over the town. It was as if they didn't see it, as if it was nothing more than the trickle that was always there.

"We should get to high ground," I said to Rob as he and Audrey passed by.

Rob ignored me, but Audrey smiled reassuringly. "It's just a spring shower."

"No, it's not."

But they went on. I caught Cassandra by the arm as she lifted her skirts to navigate one of the rapidly-growing puddles. "It's not safe here in town," I told her.

She smiled at me, then glanced away and walked on.

Couldn't they see, didn't they want to see? Why didn't they want to see?

I jumped the torrent and ran toward Chesaw Street. I reached Amy's house just as she stepped out. "Amy, we've got to get out of here, get to higher ground."

"I missed you last night," she said.

"Yeah, I know, I'm sorry. Listen to me. There's going to be a flash flood, it's going to wipe out the town, we've got to get to high ground."

"I know, Dan." She took my arm. But when I tried to head up Chesaw Street to the top of the hill, she headed the other way. Into town.

"Didn't you hear me?" I demanded.

She sighed. "I heard you."

I wanted to throw her over my shoulder and haul her off. "Then come on!"

Her shoulders slumped. It was as if all the spark of life had gone out of her. "We need to get to church, Dan."

"We need to get to high ground!"

She let go of my arm. "You've made your choice, haven't you?"

"What?!"

But all she did was stand on tiptoe and kiss me gently on the lips, then turn away and head into town.

I stood, frozen, and watched her till she turned the corner onto Okanogan Avenue.

No. I had to try again, not just for Amy, but for the whole town. I couldn't just give up on all of them, not after they'd given me so much. I couldn't let the flood kill them all – again? still? I couldn't let Max, whoever he was, whatever he was, do this to them. Could I change things? Change the history of this town? And if I did, what would happen?

It didn't matter. I had to try. I turned and ran toward the church.

CHAPTER 22

The church bell had stopped ringing. As I approached the white-steepled building that looked like it belonged in New England, not eastern Washington, I could hear voices singing. I recognized the tune. Anybody would. The last time I'd heard *Amazing Grace*, I thought ironically, had been a bagpipe version just before I graduated from the academy, at the funeral of one of my fellow highway patrol officers who'd been hit by a car during a routine traffic stop.

I strode into the vestibule and opened the door into the sanctuary. The lyrics suddenly became clear and sharp, as if someone had turned up the volume. "When we've been here ten thousand years... bright shining as the sun. We've no less days to sing God's praise... than when we first begun."

The God Carol had tried to teach me about would have hated this place and everything it stood for. Trying to escape Heaven – or *was* this place Heaven? It had certainly been everything I'd ever wanted, being needed, being liked, being useful. Even the possibility of love. Belonging. All the things I'd wanted for so long. Did God approve, or was Max– I snorted. Max was no god. He was an evil little man who'd somehow managed to trap these people into something like

Groundhog Day, and he was never going to let them go. Worse, he was dragging new people into his scheme just to keep it going. Evil didn't begin to describe it. No matter how heaven-like it was.

The hymn was over and an expectant hush had fallen over the crowd. When I let go of the door and it fell shut behind me every face turned to look. Not surprised, then. I should have known.

I took a deep breath. "People. There's a flood coming. You've got to get out of here to higher ground. Now."

Max – of course Max. Who else would be acting as preacher as well as de facto mayor and puppeteer? He stood at the pulpit, smiling benevolently down at me.

"Isn't anybody listening?" I said desperately. "There's a flood coming, dammit."

"We know, Daniel," Max said. I stared around the congregation. They were all nodding. "Through many troubles, toils, and snares, we have already come."

I wanted to snarl. "Don't quote the damned hymnal at me."

Belinda stood and glared at me. "You will watch your language in the house of the Lord."

"It's all right," Max said. "He's upset. That's how he expresses himself when he's upset."

"It is not all right," Belinda said gruffly, but she sat down.

"I'm sorry, Belinda," I said stiffly. "It's more important that we get out of here. The water is coming."

"Yes, it is," Max said. "Listen."

I could hear it then. A dull roar, off in the distance, sounding like a semi working its way over Snoqualmie Pass. "Oh, God," I said, and it wasn't a swearword.

"Have you changed your mind, then, Daniel?" Max asked softly. The rest of the room had gone utterly quiet. Not motionless, not like last night, thank God for small favors. I could hear them breathing, a great sigh in and out, and in the silence I could hear Patsy Fogle shushing little Betsy. "If not, you'd better get going quickly."

"Please," I said, and put all my heart and soul into it. "Please, come with me. All of you." I stared around at these people I had come to – love, dammit. Then I saw Amy sitting at the end of one of the pews and strode up to her. Reached out for her hand. "Amy. You of all people–"

"I, of all people, am staying, Danny." She smiled at me, but her eyes were sad. And she kept her hands in her lap and didn't rise. "If you're going, please go now. I won't ask you to stay, even though that's what I want more than anything."

The roar was getting louder. More like a train approaching the station now.

I stared down at her. I wanted to pick her up and carry her off but I knew she'd fight me, and so would everyone else if I tried. "I can't."

She nodded understanding. "I know. Go. While you still can."

"You're insane. You're all insane." I turned and ran down the aisle, through the vestibule, out the door. Looked up the street. "Oh, shit." It was a helluva lot closer than I'd thought it would be. A solid wall of water, whole trees, mud, dead animals, and God knows what else. And it was headed straight down Okanogan Avenue, taking out everything in its path.

I ran around the church to the hill and scrambled up it, bashing through blackberries and sagebrush, between bright green larch and maple trees. I tripped and fell twice. The first time I landed on my face. I yanked myself up, swiped at the blood streaming from my nose, and kept going. The second time my right knee landed cockeyed on a rock and twisted. I felt something pop, but I pulled myself up in spite of the tearing pain, and kept going until I'd reached the top, where I collapsed on the ground, wheezing, as if all my strings had been cut.

I squeezed my eyes shut against the devastation, against the loss. I curled up into a ball, hugging my knee. Something was badly wrong there. And my hand, the one I'd sprained in the wreck that had brought me here in the first place, was aching like I'd really broken it this time. My head was ringing like the church bell.

No, that *was* the church bell, clanging like a madman was swinging on the rope. I couldn't think of anything I wanted to do less at that moment than look at the devastation below, the loss of the only people I'd had in my life who'd made me happy since my mother left.

But when I finally screwed up my courage and opened my eyes, raised my head and squinted into the light, what I saw was even worse.

The sun. Was shining. The grass. Was lush. The blackberries were blooming and the larches were covered in pale new spring green needles.

And the town of Conconully was a few piles of splintered silver planks, bits of broken glass glinting like diamonds in the knee-high weeds covering what had once been a bustling main street. Salmon Creek was a few pools of water in an otherwise dry streambed. The church was completely gone. The mercantile building was the only one left standing, its roof half caved in and its windows broken out. That damned plaster pig was gazing through the remaining splinters, leaning drunkenly on the half-gone platform floorboards. I swear it had a grin on its face.

The flood was a hundred and twenty years ago, I thought dizzily. It's not 1894 anymore. Amy.

Pools of black swirled like floodwater in front of my eyes, thick and gluey. I put my head back down on my good knee as they spread out over my field of vision. Dry heaved my empty stomach.

That's the last thing I remember. Will ever remember. Will ever want to remember.

CHAPTER 23

Of course, it wasn't the last thing I remembered, no matter how badly I'd wanted it to be.

The first thing I noticed when I got back to the point of noticing things again, sort of, was the smell. Antiseptic and sterile, cold and sharp. Modern. No herbal tang of arnica or bitter reek of willow bark. I couldn't recognize this odor, didn't want to recognize it. So I ignored it. It wouldn't go away, but I didn't have to pay attention to it.

Some time later, I don't know how long, I started to notice the sounds. Rhythmic beeps, mostly. Mechanical. Unrelenting. Sometimes they went faster, sometimes slower. Sometimes they made a rhythm like a waltz. One-two-three, one-two-three. I didn't want them to do that, and wished they'd just go away, but they never did. One-two-three, one-two-three. The beat made me want to cry, but I couldn't remember how.

More sounds. Steps. First they'd get louder, then stop, then they'd start up again and get softer, then fade away altogether. I was glad when they faded away.

It was a long time before I felt the hands, but once I did they were relentless, too. They made me aware of my body for the first time. Of legs and arms and torso. And head. And skin. Rough skin, soft skin, cloths and wet and dry. And pain. I shied back from the pain and sank away from the hands into a place where I couldn't even hear the beeps.

Solitude. No one could hurt me there.

* * *

It couldn't last, though. The hands came back, and they brought voices with them. None of them were familiar, and I couldn't understand the sounds. Didn't want to. But I couldn't make them go away this time, and eventually words started popping out and forcing me to understand them. "wake" and "dying?" That last one sounded like pain. I ignored it. "coma" "someday" Someday a long way off, I hoped. "damage" What damage? Why did they care?

Eventually the voices went away. I could hear the steps fading and a door closing.

A long while later, I noticed the light. It wasn't That Light, beckoning me down a long tunnel or anything. It was just a glare against my eyelids. I could feel it warm on my face.

For the first time, I wanted to open my eyes. See Amy. Amy? Where had that name come from? Then I remembered, and screwed my eyelids tighter to keep the nonexistent tears in.

"Jim, did you see that?"

A whole sentence. Damn. See what, I wondered? Not me. I didn't do anything. Jim? Oh, Dad. What was he doing here? Had they made him have an accident, too?

"Yeah. I did." Something came closer, blocking the light. I wanted that light back. "Dan?" The voice, a suddenly familiar voice, came from much closer. "Dan, can you hear me?"

That wasn't the right question. The right question was did I want to hear him, and the answer was no.

"I swear I saw him squeeze his eyes shut."

Another hand on my arm. I knew that hand. I wanted to shake it off. "I saw it, too. I'll go get the doctor."

Oh, yes, please, I thought. Please go get Doc Amy. I'll wake up for her, I promise.

But the voice Carol went and got wasn't Amy's. I wanted to tell her, tell her what? To go get a dead woman? No matter how much I needed her? The strange man touched me and took my pulse and lifted one of my eyelids and said, "I wouldn't be surprised if it's soon now." Then his steps faded away.

I could hear Dad and Carol talking softly above me, but the words wore me out and I fell back into the welcome darkness again.

* * *

The next time I noticed something, I was alone. Don't ask me how I knew. It was dark, or at least the lights were out. My hand hurt, and my knee hurt, and my head hurt. But I was awake, and there wasn't a damned thing I could do about it.

I took a chance, and opened my eyes. White walls dimmed to gray in the dark room. Tiny multicolored lights glowed from a machine to the side of my bed, and that's where the beeping was coming from, too. I wished I could smash the beeping, but both of my hands were so heavy it felt like they'd tied weights to them.

The window was uncovered to the rain mixed with snow dripping down the glass. Still raining. Flood. That hurt worse than my head and knee combined. I wanted to forget.

The overhead light flashed on. I snapped my eyes shut against the glare.

"Dan?" Steps rapid across the room. "Dan? Are you awake?"

Crap. She'd seen me. I lay still, hoping she'd go away, but she didn't.

"Dan? Open your eyes for me please, Dan."

"No." My voice sounded like I hadn't spoken in months. Maybe I hadn't.

"Oh, Daniel." Arms went around me and a face pressed itself to mine. A wet face. Then it lifted, and Carol called out, "Jim! Come here! He's awake!"

* * *

Well, that was the end of that. By the end of the week, whether I wanted to or not, they were making me sit up in bed and eat hospital food, which tasted like something Audrey wouldn't have fed the cat. And making me let them run test after test. And answer question after question.

I asked a few of my own, but they wouldn't tell me enough. Just that they'd used my cell phone – my smashed cell phone? – to triangulate my location, and I'd been found within hours. That I'd been airlifted to Harborview Medical Center in Seattle because of my head injury, and I'd been in a coma for days. Just days?

I had more visitors than I knew what to do with, more people who thought they knew me than I'd known existed. People from Carol's church. People I'd known at the academy. Even Sergeant MacKade came all the way over from the highway patrol office in Omak, although she was mainly there to get the information to finish her reports. She only smiled and shook her head at me when I mentioned coming back to work soon, and I realized they'd probably already filled my job. No excuses to go back. It was probably just as well.

It set up an ache no amount of oxycodone could get rid of.

Another week, and they were ready to discharge me. I was making a better recovery, they said, than anyone had hoped for. My broken hand just needed time to be as good as new. My knee could finish mending at home, too. It would never be the same, but, if I was diligent about my physical therapy, they hoped I'd eventually be able to work down to just a cane. The head injury was healing well, too.

The only thing that wasn't healing was my soul, and there wasn't anything they could do about that.

"Damn Max and his damned choices."

My timing could have been better. Carol looked up from where she was settling me in on their living room couch. "Who? What choices?"

I shook my head. "Never mind."

But Carol being Carol, of course, she couldn't let it go. "Is Max someone you met over in Omak?"

What else could I say? "Yeah."

"What was he trying to make you choose?" She eyed me. I'd have laughed if it hadn't hurt too much.

"He was just a friend." Well, the last thing he'd been was my friend, but he certainly wasn't the conclusion she'd jumped to, either. I added, for good measure, "I don't swing that way."

"I'm glad to hear that. Not," she added, "because there's anything wrong with it, mind you."

Maybe so, but it still made her uncomfortable. And the fact that she'd felt like she had to ask... God. Nobody knew me here.

Not Dad, whose hours in the evenings he spent with me were just about as awkward; or my young half-siblings, who popped in and out more to stare than to keep me company; or the few friends I'd had on this side of the mountains. Not even Linda, who came over one afternoon to "see if you want some company."

I blame her visit on Carol, because when I didn't immediately tell Linda I loved her and had missed her and especially when I didn't beg her to stay, she stiffened right up and told me she'd come back when I was feeling better. That was the last I saw of her, in spite of Carol's hints that I ought to call her.

The only thing that mattered was the physical therapy. Carol drove me down three times a week, and I pushed and grunted and stretched and pulled. The therapist was ninety-five percent really nice middle-aged lady, and five per cent sadist. When I told her so, she laughed and said it was a job requirement. When I told her I appreciated the fact, she chuckled again.

At least I could amuse someone else, even through the pain. If I could make her laugh then she didn't look at me with worry in her eyes. Everybody did, when they thought I wasn't paying attention. The doctor threatened to send me to a mental health counselor if I didn't shape up. So if I could make at least one person think I wanted to be where I was, well, maybe she'd pass the word along.

And her goal was the same as mine. I wanted on my feet. Both feet. Walking. And I wasn't giving up till I got there. Because the sooner I was walking, the sooner I could get out of Dad and Carol's house. My plans pretty much stopped there, but it was enough.

* * *

I don't think it was a coincidence that my last session with the physical therapist was in May. Spring was coming on, the rain was down to the occasional shower, and it was staying daylight till almost nine o'clock. Carol's irises were in bloom. I'd always loved Carol's irises, but this year they looked gray and blurry. Everything looked gray and blurry. Everything had ever since I'd left Conconully.

I walked carefully up the uneven flagstone walkway to Dad and Carol's house, trying to use the cane as little as possible. Nowadays I could get away without it almost entirely indoors, where there were handy walls if I needed to lean on something, but outdoors it was still a necessity.

I'd been able to get behind the wheel for over a month now. Dad had managed to bring my car, along with all my other possessions, back from Omak while I was recovering, so I had that much independence, at least. Against Dad's wishes, I'd contacted Sergeant MacKade about coming back to work, but I'd been right that she'd replaced me. It hadn't come as a shock. With only ten troopers out of the Omak office covering over five thousand square miles of Okanogan County, she couldn't afford to let my job stay open for long. Or to give me desk work till I could pass the physicals again. Assuming I'd ever be able to.

Dad was after me to put my name back in the applicant pool for somewhere on this side of the mountains, but the same applied, with the added disadvantage that nobody over here knew me from Adam. Besides, I didn't want to stay on this side of the mountains.

It was time. It was past time. I knew what I wanted. I had my health back, or as much of it as I was likely to get. I could drive. I could walk if you didn't want me to go hiking in the mountains. I could think straight, Dad's opinion notwithstanding.

The house was empty. Carol had left a note saying she'd gone shopping. The kids were at school. Dad was at work. I went to the guest room, my old room that hadn't ever seemed like mine, and yanked my duffel bag off the top shelf of the closet. After I put everything I needed into it, it was less than half full. I pulled my cell phone out of my pocket, turned it off, and left it in the bottom dresser drawer. With any luck, they wouldn't realize I didn't have it on me until it was too late. Too late for what, I didn't know.

I left a note on the kitchen table. Bye, thanks, basically. God knows what they'd think when they found it. I didn't think it'd surprise them. I hoped it wouldn't send them chasing after me.

I locked the front door behind me, and left the house key under the mat. Duffel over my shoulder, I worked my way back down the front walk.

I climbed into my car and headed for I-90. Eastbound.

CHAPTER 24

It takes about five hours to get to the Okanogan from west Seattle. Over the mountains and through the woods. The rain began around North Bend and poured until I topped out over Snoqualmie Pass, where it shut off like someone had thrown a switch. The sun came out, and I tipped down the visor. I turned north at Cle Elum and climbed up and over Blewett Pass, then down into the canyon of the Wenatchee River.

I'd never seen the east side of the mountains so green before. Apple trees full of blossoms floated like clouds over the hillsides, and swept down to the river as the land opened out. The sky was the most incredible deep blue, and the air was dry. I could breathe it. It was the first time I'd felt like I could breathe since I woke up in the hospital.

I crossed the Columbia River above Wenatchee and headed north again, following the wide open river valley. Saw a hawk dive from a power line, and half a dozen deer grazing along the fence keeping them out of the apple orchards. Drove past the sign for Fort Okanogan, the early 19th century trading post. I'd always meant to come down and go through the museum there, but I'd never had the chance. No time or desire now.

The traffic thinned out more the farther I left Wenatchee behind. The road, and the land, opened up even further. Space. So much space. I saw a house, perched on the high hillside, its narrow gravel road winding like a snake from the highway. Another. And another. A truck ground its way up one of the narrow tracks, leaving a trail of dust in its wake.

I left the Columbia River at Bridgeport, crossing the Okanogan River on its namesake bridge before following the smaller river northwestward. Small towns and more orchards, these not quite in bloom yet, flitted past. I wasn't paying attention, was rubbing my knee with one hand while I pushed down on the gas with my other foot, when I saw blue flashing lights behind me. I sighed and pulled over.

The cruiser looked familiar. So did the officer who got out of the car.

"Sergeant."

"Reilly." She didn't look surprised. Neither was I. "What are you doing on this side of the mountains?"

"Taking a drive."

She leaned over to peer in the window. "You're a long way from home."

Not as far as I had been, I thought. "I needed to get away for a little while."

"Your family's worried about you."

"I know. It's why I needed to get away."

She shook her head. "That's not what I meant."

I sighed. "They call in a missing persons on me? I've only been gone a few hours."

"Not officially. They said you left a note."

I didn't know what to say to that, and it wasn't any of her business, anyway. I shrugged.

She let out her breath in a huff. "You going to call them or will I have to?"

"I will." Eventually. Or never.

A car whooshed by, and she waited until the sound had faded before she said, "Maybe I'll just give them a call, too."

"Why? Don't you trust me?"

It was her turn to shrug. "Not particularly. Not after what I saw of you in the hospital, and especially not after what I heard from your parents not an hour ago."

"I'll call." I'd tell her anything to get away.

"Why don't you do it right now?" She pulled out a cell phone and tried to hand it to me.

I shook my head and lied. "I'll do it later."

Now she sounded exasperated. Well, so was I. "I can't make you. I can't make you do anything. I'm just saying it's not fair to worry your family like that again."

"Okay." I started the engine.

She stepped back. "You were a good officer."

"I'm not an officer anymore." Oddly enough, I didn't care.

She nodded. "I'm sorry about that."

"I'm sorry, too." I shifted the car into drive.

"Don't do anything foolish."

I put my foot on the gas, and left her behind.

* * *

Omak was a blur, the small-town traffic simply an obstacle, and I almost missed the turn. I'd thought about getting some lunch, but I wasn't hungry. I wasn't much of anything, and I didn't know what I was going to do when I got wherever the hell I was going.

Conconully. There wasn't going to be anything there, besides a few tumbledown buildings and that damned pig, even if it was still there, which wasn't likely. I knew the pig wasn't going to be able to take me back, even if I found it. I told myself, as I headed west out of town toward the mountains, I wasn't stupid enough to think I was going to try.

That wasn't the point. I didn't know or care what the point was by then, so I concentrated on what I could do. Fourteen more miles, winding up the bench out of the broad valley of the Okanogan River.

I pulled over at the viewpoint at the top, and gazed back down the valley. Started to get out of the car, then thought better of the idea when my knee nearly buckled under me. Five hours in the car without a stop hadn't been good for it, even if it had been good for me. So I sat, and looked through the open window, and smelled the sweet sage and apple blossom, and wondered how this part of the world had got to feel like where I belonged.

But I didn't belong here anymore, and home was somewhere I could never go again. Still, at least this place smelled the same, looked the same, felt the same.

I took a deep breath. "After I'm done —" how? with what? "— I'll go back down to Omak, and, and —" I couldn't finish the sentence. And do what? Look for work? But I couldn't have what I wanted, and, well, there was only one other alternative.

I started the car and nudged it back up on the road. The sooner I proved Conconully had been nothing but a figment of my brain-damaged imagination, the sooner I could try to let go of it. One way or the other.

As I drove on, I started to wonder if I'd even know where to go to find the ruins again. It wasn't as if I'd been paying attention the first time I'd arrived there, and it wasn't as if I'd left under my own steam. Or even my own consciousness. But I had a general idea, and the landmarks were beginning to look familiar.

I had plenty of time. I could explore every damned dirt road in the county if I had to. But I wasn't there. Not yet.

As it turned out, I didn't need to worry about not being able to find it. I just knew. Even if it didn't look like I remembered it.

Oh, the road, the curve I'd almost missed chasing Audrey's truck, and the trees I'd nearly sideswiped that night last November were there, but the turnoff itself was chewed up like a parade of tractors had been driving up and down it for a month. I sat, staring at the mud and the tracks and the scars on the trees unfortunate enough to be too close to where heavy equipment had obviously plowed through.

This couldn't be it. But it was.

As I sat there in the middle of the road, a backhoe came up behind me and blasted its horn. I pulled over to the side of the road, and watched as it lurched down the dirt track toward Conconully.

I needed to know. I simply had to know. And if I drove my car over the cliff again? It was that other alternative. Suicide had been at the back of my mind ever since I'd realized I was still alive, and the only way I'd survived this long was a promise to myself I'd get back here before I even thought about doing anything – "foolish" – as the Sergeant had said.

Keep going, I told myself. Don't think. You're only here to see what's what, one more time. I eased the car down onto the dirt track, and began bumping my way along.

It would have been a lousy place to try to kill myself, anyway. Kind of hard to wreck the car when my maximum speed was less than five miles an hour. Not that I couldn't have gunned the engine, but I'm pretty sure all that would have done was spin my wheels into the mud. So I crept along, more sure I was on the right road with every foot forward.

But when I passed the canyon, and came around the last bend, I stopped the car dead in its tracks to stare at a construction site. At least three backhoes and shovels, half a dozen dump trucks, and twenty or more men in or on or around them.

And where the ghost town – and the real town – of Conconully was supposed to be, a sheet of clear water reflected the sky.

I parked the car in a level spot out of the way, and, slowly, my knee aching like a son of a gun, managed to gimp my way out.

"Can I help you?"

The man was wearing a hard hat, a flannel shirt, muddy blue jeans, and equally muddy boots. I'm not sure what I was expecting, but I was incredibly glad he was a total stranger. If he'd looked the least bit like Max I'm not sure what I'd have done.

"Can I help you?" he repeated.

I waved an arm in the general direction of the mess. "What's going on?"

He looked surprised, but said, "We're taking out the dam."

"Why?"

"Salmon habitat. This was a spawning stream for an endangered run of coho. We're trying to bring it back to what it used to be. Bring the salmon back, get the run going again."

"Oh."

"I'm going to have to ask you to leave," he went on. "Unless you've got official permission to be here."

"No," I said. No point in trying to fool him. He was already fishing in his pocket, probably hunting for his cell phone. "No, I don't." I glanced around, and thought faster than I had in months. I had to stay. I had to see. I pointed on up the road a piece, to where it came over the rise on the way to the historical marker. "Would it matter if I watched from there? I've never seen anything like this before."

He looked dubious.

"I'll stay out of the way, I promise."

"You will if you don't want to get washed away. I can't say I like the idea."

"You'll never know I'm there."

"Right." He looked like he was about to tell me "no" in no uncertain terms, then gave me a hard glance. "Oh, go ahead. Just stay the hell out of the way."

"I will."

I left before he could change his mind, but I could feel him watching me as I limped back to my car and climbed in.

I started the engine, put the car in drive and pushed on the gas. I could hear the engine roar and feel the wheels spinning in the mud, but the car just sat there. Great. If I was going to be a pain in the ass, he'd probably change his mind and chase me off anyhow.

If he could. His face appeared at my window. I rolled it down, and he said, "I'll count to three and give you a shove. You put on the gas again."

"Thanks."

He strolled around to the back of my car. "One. Two. Three!"

I pumped the gas. He shoved. The car moved. "Thanks!" I yelled out, and rolled the window closed before he could tell me to keep going back to the highway.

I crept up the hill all the way to the top, praying I wouldn't get stuck again the whole time, and pulled the car out of the way of any more machinery that might be coming.

Then, conscious of being watched, I climbed out of the car again, grabbed the damned cane, and edged slowly around the car till I could lean against the hood. I waved at the construction guy, like a good civilian. He waved in return, then went back to work.

I leaned on the hood for a few more minutes, gathering my strength. Or maybe it was my courage. Or something. I could see the whole works from here. Two enormous front-end shovels were scooping from an ever-increasing hole in this side of the dam. I could see the earth of the dam weakening.

If I was going to do this...

I didn't want to take the cane, but I didn't have a choice. No way was I going to be able to get down the hill, through that patch of trees, and around behind where the shovels were digging without something to lean on.

I had to see, at least. Or maybe more. I had to see where the townsite was, see if I could find something, anything to prove I hadn't dreamed it all. Maybe I could find that damned pig. I shook my head and lurched my way down the slope, swearing under my breath, staying behind rocks and anything else I could find to hide me.

When I finally reached the bottom, and the trees, the going got easier. Sort of. At least I wasn't having to crouch to hide, not that my knee could bother to appreciate the difference. It felt like it was on fire.

I kept going, anyway. Through the woods, past the shovels, upstream to –

"Hey, you! Watch out!"

I ignored him.

"Damn you! Get out of there!"

I looked back. They were coming after me. I watched them coming toward me, but I didn't move. I knew they weren't going to get to me in time. I knew I wasn't going to make it, and I didn't care. I stood directly in front of the dam now. The cracks in the dam were widening, dark crevasses the color of chocolate under the pale gray gravel surface. I was tempted to walk into one...

The water, when it came, was loaded with sticks and mud and rocks. It wasn't gentle. It burst through those cracks like it was carving a new landscape. I watched it heading toward me, time stretching out into a place where it didn't exist anymore, where I could fall back into that place where I could hear nothing, feel nothing, see nothing.

The water filled my eyes, my nose, my mouth. My lungs. Snatched my cane out of my hand. Yanked my feet out from under me. Battered my body till I went limp, and then flung me around like a wet towel. Thumped my head against something hard enough to knock me out. Swept me away.

CHAPTER 25

When I came to, it felt like I'd broken every bone in my body. For all I knew, I had. I was lying in earth's biggest mud puddle, cold water oozing up into hair and clothes already soaking wet, the sun beating down against me, probably raising steam. I opened my eyes and stared around.

"Oh, shit." Which was the understatement of the century. It hadn't worked. Stupid, harebrained scheme, idiotic, imbecilic– It had been a dream, part of the coma, part of the world I was stuck in for the rest of my life.

I lay there, wishing I knew swearwords adequate to the purpose, waiting – for what, now? For the construction guys to haul me out of the mud, read me the riot act, send me home, probably.

I closed my eyes and wished the flood had had the good sense to kill me once and for all.

* * *

Nobody came. After a little while, I wiggled my arms and legs, and discovered nothing was broken after all. Bruised and wrenched, yes, and my knee was pretty pissed at me, but not as bad as it could have been. I levered myself to my elbows and looked around at the slowly drying mud stretching out to a sharp line on the hillsides.

No use staying here. I sat up. My cane was gone – for good, I suspected. At any rate, I wasn't going to spend the time looking for it. I struggled to my feet and limped upstream, so to speak, figuring the construction guys had to be near where the dam had been. My car was in that direction, too.

I'd been swept a long way down the streambed, or at least that's what it seemed like. It was a never-ending, never-changing sea of mud and uprooted trees and sheared-off cliff faces. I knew water was destructive, but it's not really possible to know how much damage it can do till you see it for yourself. I thought about Conconully's original flood, and shivered. Well, I was shivering from the breeze against my slowly drying clothes, too, but not just.

The damage was so – complete. How could those construction guys let this happen? What if there'd been people downstream? I suppose if there had been they wouldn't have done it this way, but it still seemed counterproductive if they were trying to restore the creek for the salmon.

I wasn't making much sense by then. My knee ached, although not as badly as it had, and so did my hand, but my head felt like it had been rattled around in a cement mixer. I didn't dare look back to see my progress, such as it was, for fear of losing sight of the goal altogether.

The climb got steeper. The mud began to dry out a bit, which was good as I felt like I had concrete overshoes on instead of my boots. I stopped to clunk them against a downed tree to loosen the load, which helped some.

But not enough. The sun was getting low. Pretty soon it would go over the edge of the mountains altogether, and I'd be out here in the dark. No flashlight, no cell phone, of course.

No cell phone? I reached into my pocket, then remembered I'd left it at Dad and Carol's on purpose. Thinking I was going to find a way to go back to a place where a cell phone wouldn't do me any good.

Idiot wasn't a strong enough word for who I was, out here looking for the impossible dream I'd had. I made my way over to the edge of the mudflow, found myself a downed tree, and sat. Watched the sun set over the mountains, and dusk fall. And the stars come out. Finally, I sank down with my back to the tree, put my head on my knees, and, in spite of everything, fell asleep.

* * *

"Here's Tim! We've got everybody, right?" The voice, female, sounded familiar. Not Carol, not, thank God, Linda, but who?

Oh, good, I thought muzzily. I'm dreaming again. I wonder if I'm back in Harborview in another coma, or if they've given up on me altogether and I'm still out here dying.

It didn't matter. I struggled to my feet. Can't be a dream if I hurt this much still, right? Well, no, that hadn't held true the last time.

"Good. Let's go." A man. Familiar again, but not Dad, not – No. I knew that voice. But that meant I was dreaming, or it *was* real...

"All right." I recognized that one, too.

But the voices were fading, as if they were walking away.

"Wait for me!" I yelled. "Don't leave!" I took one step, then another and another. Before I knew it I was hurtling up the hill.

I could hear them. I could tell they'd stopped. And another voice. I recognized that one. "Did you hear something?"

"Audrey, wait!"

"Is that–? Just a minute."

"I thought we had everybody."

I was close, I was so close. "Don't go!"

I fell over something. No, not just something. I felt the plaster that wasn't plaster, the snout, the tail, the ears. It was the damned pig, and I wrapped my arms around it. "I've got Harry!!" I yelled.

I could hear the gasps, and they weren't just from climbing the hill. I could see dozens of lanterns now, flickering in the dusk like they had that very first night. The whole town must be out here, I realized, but of course they would be. The whole town. *My* whole town. "Here! Come here!"

They pelted toward me, lanterns bobbing.

"Sheriff?" That *was* Audrey, wasn't it?

"Sheriff Reilly?" *And* Rob.

"Daniel?" Max sounded more shocked than relieved like the others, but –

"Danny, is that you?"

"Amy!" I never thought I'd be so glad to hear that voice. I blinked.

And there they were.

Afterword

Thank you for reading *Sojourn*. I hope you enjoyed it. Reviews help other readers find books. I appreciate all reviews, whether positive or negative.

Sojourn is based on a real place, and real events. However, the actual Conconully, Washington, is not a ghost town but a going concern, kept alive these days chiefly by tourists. The 1894 flood did happen, and the historical marker documenting that flood is real, too. Harry the pig's prototype exists, in the person of a plaster swine housed in the display window of a building very like Conconully's mercantile, but located in Molson, Washington, a tiny half ghost town, half living hamlet just south of the Canadian border. All of the geographical names are real as well, even if some of them are used to describe places that aren't where they should be. Everything else is a figment of my imagination.

If you're interested in reading more about the actual history behind *Sojourn*, please go to the Pathfinders pages at http://mmjustus.com, where I have put together a bibliography of books and websites about the Okanogan Country and its history. My photos pages at the same site house a collection of snapshots of locations in the story, along with one of Harry the pig.

Would you like to know when my next book is available? You can sign up for my new release email list at http://mmjustus.com, or follow me on on Facebook https://www.facebook.com/M.M.Justusauthor, or at Twitter @mmjustus.

Sojourn is the first of my Tales of the Unearthly Northwest. You might also enjoy my Time in Yellowstone series, a set of primarily historical novels (with just a little time travel) set mostly in and around Yellowstone National Park.

If you would like to read an excerpt from *Reunion,* the second Tale, please turn the page.

LOST IN TIME

The year is 1910, and unemployed teacher Claudia Ogden is at the end of her rope. With nowhere to go and no one to rely on, she has no future at all. Hearing a rumor of a job in a small, remote town called Conconully, she decides to bet what's left of her life on it.

But when she arrives, and is hired, to her relief, what at first seem like small eccentricities loom ever larger and more inexplicably, mysteries that make no sense. That is, until she meets Conconully's accidental magician, who wants *her* to save *them*.

But from what?

Chapter 1

"Please, Miss Ogden, sit down." The principal's voice was kindly but sad, as was her smile, If I hadn't already known the news was going to be bad simply because I had been called into her office, it was as certain now as the pain. And that pain was a fact of life. Had been since before I'd taken this new job in Seattle, almost a year ago now. But it had worsened to the point that I'd missed days of classes, unable to rise from my bed. Too many days. Which was why I was here, now, sitting in Miss Taylor's office, waiting to be told they'd have to let me go.

"Have you seen a doctor?"

"Yes." I had finally, at Jean's insistence, used the money I owed her for rent and made an appointment, for all the good it had done me. Now I was in debt to her and no better off for it. Worse off, given what was about to happen to me.

"Was he able to discern what the problem is?" Perhaps she was hoping I'd tell her he was curing me. Maybe she wanted to keep me. If nothing else, it would save her the trouble of hiring someone else.

But no. Dr. Spencer had been useless to me, for all he'd tried to hide the fact. I'd seen it in his eyes. I swallowed. "I-it's female troubles, ma'am."

Her face grew grim. "You're not with child, are you?"

My breath left me in a whoosh of a "No!" But her expression did not change, and I could feel the hopelessness settling into my soul along with the pain that even now was making it difficult to keep my back straight and not bend me over. I shook my head, to add to the emphasis. If only that was the problem. But whatever trouble was in my womb, the doctor could not determine what it was, and could not do anything.

"Will you be well soon?"

I shrugged helplessly. "I don't know. The doctor doesn't know, either."

Her brow furrowed. "Will you be going to a specialist?"

Dr. Spencer had broached the subject, but I could not afford it, not on a teacher's salary. "No, ma'am."

Miss Taylor's expression faded into something resembling pity. I supposed I did seem pitiful to her, but I could not muster the dignity to deny it.

"You have missed six days in the last month, and more than two weeks since term began two months ago." She paused, as if she didn't want to do what I, or my illness, had forced her to do. "I am sorry, Miss Ogden."

I blinked my stinging eyes, determined not to shame myself in front of her. Not any more than I already had. "Yes, I know. I will gather my things."

I had reached the door and put my hand on the knob when she said, "You are one of the best teachers I've ever had the pleasure to work with. I wish you well, Miss Ogden."

At least I made it out of the building before the tears began to fall.

* * *

"That witch!" Jean exclaimed. "Why not kick you to the gutter as well as knocking you down?"

"It was not her fault." I sank into one of the two armchairs flanking the fireplace. The parlor of the little house in west Seattle I shared with my friend and landlady was a warm and cozy space.

Three steps took Jean across the room. She turned back to face me. "They have an obligation to help you, Claudia, not to make things worse."

I stared at her. I should have expected something like this from Jean, whose thoughts on the subject of employee/employer relations put her somewhere on the far side of the radical Wobblies. The Industrial Workers of the World had caused a general strike in Seattle a few years ago, and, from what I understood, had not accomplished a thing besides bringing the city to a standstill. But I had not expected it. I had expected her to take my side, and be sympathetic, and do all the normal things one's friends do when one stumbles over misfortune. But no. She had to make even my illness someone else's responsibility.

"The district cannot afford to keep a teacher who is too ill to teach."

"Then they should pay for the care that will make you well again. Your principal said you are the best teacher she's ever worked with."

I should not have told Jean that, but it was the one bright spot in this awful day. "One of the best, yes." I could not help smiling.

She did not smile back at me. "And yet she let you go because you are too ill to work. Have you made an appointment with that specialist yet?"

I did not reply, but she apparently saw my answer in my face, because her frown deepened into a scowl. "If you do not, I shall do it for you."

"Jean—"

But she rode right over me. "What was his name? Dr. Whittington?"

"Jean—"

But she was already on the telephone, speaking with the operator. While I wished I had the strength, or the determination, to stop her, I sank back in the chair in defeat.

* * *

She went with me, too. "To make sure you don't back out," she told me. Jean was a good friend. Bossy and overbearing and thoroughly convinced she always knew best, but a good friend. And when the appointment was over, and payment was mentioned, she glared me down and produced the cash herself.

It wasn't charity, I told myself. But it was. And I was so beaten down by what the specialist had told me I let her do it. She knew my situation from that alone, even though I'd been fighting to keep my despair from my face the moment I walked out of the examining room. The doctor had performed enough humiliating and, as it turned out, unnecessary scrutiny to tell me what my heart had already known before I left Montana last year. After all, wasn't that the main reason I'd left in the first place? Perhaps not the main reason, as I had wanted the adventure, and to relieve my parents of one more burden as well. After all, my intellect, such as it was, had refused to believe what my heart knew until I could ignore it no longer.

Jean did not say anything until we reached our house – her house, really, as I was simply her tenant as well as her friend, and would not be either, or anything, much longer – and the door closed behind us.

She waited, until I fell more than sat into that same wing chair where she'd bullied me into going to the appointment where I'd heard

234

my sentence. Then she said, more gently than I'd ever heard her before, "That bad, is it?"

I nodded, tried to speak, couldn't, and she sank down on the arm of the chair, putting a warm arm around me. "I am so sorry, my dear." She leaned away from me, as if ashamed of her kindness, and added in a tone more like herself, "What will you do now?"

Because of course I could not batten on her charity forever. "I don't know. Go home, I guess."

"You are home," she told me firmly.

It was kind of her, but no. "I meant Montana." Not that I could batten on my family, either. They could not afford to take me in, not with six other mouths to feed and my father's work tenuous at best.

"Is that what you want?"

Of course it wasn't, and she knew it. What I wanted was my job, my home here, my friends, Jean. My normal life. But it had been snatched from me by my incurable female troubles, by this – cancer, the specialist had called it – growing in my womb. He had offered surgery, to remove it, but said it had probably already grown to other parts of my body. If I had come in when I'd first felt the pain, I might have had a chance, but now... He'd trailed off, his expression almost accusatory, as if it were my own fault I'd gotten sick, that I hadn't had the money to come see him, let alone the time and money to let him cut into me—

"No, but I cannot stay here."

"No, you can't."

Well, that was clear and sharp enough. And cold. I jerked myself up out of the chair. "I will gather my things." I had no idea where I would find the money for the train ticket, but at least my parents would be more sympathetic than this. I had thought she was my friend, no, she had been my friend. I hadn't known she was going to turn so suddenly cruel.

"No!" Jean's hand came down on my arm. "That's not what I meant and you know it."

I could not help but stare at her. Her voice was choked, and her eyes brimming. "I do not wish you to leave. I wish more than anything that you could stay."

"I-I know." And oddly enough, I did believe her. Whatever her reason for wanting me gone, I knew it was not because she did not care.

Her brows came together. Her mouth set, and she straightened her shoulders. "I know where you can go. They'll help you there." As I continued to stare at her, speechless, she told me, in the tone I'd long since learned not to even try to gainsay, "And you will go. If I have to drag you there myself."

* * *

Well, and what else could I do? I could not fight both Jean and my pain. Nor the despair born from the hopeless diagnosis the doctor had given me. The three combined to put me to bed, where I lay curled like a homunculus, breathing through the throbbing ache in my womb, unable to think, or even wonder. I heard the front door thump closed as Jean left the house.

I must have slept completely through the night in spite of everything, because the shadows were at an early morning angle through my bedroom window when I woke. Jean was standing in the doorway, a satisfied look on her face. "They'll take you," she said. "I knew they would."

"Who?" I started to ask, but she had opened the door to my wardrobe.

"Where is your valise?"

"Under the bed. Jean–"

But she was already there. "Your train leaves in two hours."

I had stared at her before, but this was sheer disbelief. "My train where?"

She dragged my valise out, opened it, and started packing my things with the practice of long experience. As an aspiring Nellie Bly – not that she called herself that but it was what she was – she was used to packing her bags on a moment's notice. It was, she'd told me when she'd first invited me to live here, why she wanted a housemate: to watch over her things and have someone living in the house while she was gone.

She glanced up at me, grinning. "Conconully."

"Conco–" I stumbled over the unfamiliar name.

"Conconully. It's a tiny place, out in the middle of nowhere, but you grew up in Montana, so that shouldn't be a problem for you. They need a schoolteacher, and have for a long time–" she hesitated briefly "–and it should suit you right down to the ground."

Startled out of my, well, startlement, I asked, "How would you know that?"

"You always told me the one thing you missed about Montana was teaching in a one-room schoolhouse instead of being nothing but a cog in a machine." She frowned. "A machine that threw you out as soon as you needed repair." The frown disappeared as she concentrated on folding another dress into my valise. "Conconully's an odd little place, but the people are friendly. It's where I grew up–" another little hesitation "–and I'd have stayed if I could, but there's no work for a journalist there." Her expression turned peculiar, then she turned back to my now-almost full valise, muttering, "except for one story, but nobody'd believe me."

"Jean, do they know about my, my–" now it was my turn to hesitate. I could not bring myself to say the words, do they know I am dying?

"Yes, they know you're ill. It's all right, Claudia." She looked up at me again, her eyes brimming. "Please, do this for me. It's all right."

And so it was that a little over two hours later, I found myself on a train headed east on the bridge over Lake Washington, away from my dearest friend, who had stuffed an assortment of tickets into my pocketbook and told the conductor to watch over me. She'd hugged me one last time and made me promise once again that I would use them all and follow her instructions to the letter.

I had promised I would. Heaven help me.

ABOUT THE AUTHOR

M.M. Justus spent most of her childhood summers in the back seat of a car, traveling with her parents to almost every national park west of the Mississippi and a great many places in between.

She holds degrees in British and American literature and history and library science, and a certificate in museum studies. In her other life, she's held jobs as far flung as hog farm bookkeeper, music school secretary, professional dilettante (aka reference librarian), and museum curator, all of which are fair fodder for her fiction.

Her other interests include quilting, gardening, meteorology, and the travel bug she inherited from her father. She lives on the rainy side of the Cascade mountains in Washington state, within easy reach of all of its mysterious places.

Please visit her website and blog at http://mmjustus.com, on Facebook at https://www.facebook.com/M.M.Justusauthor, and on Twitter @mmjustus.

Books by M.M. Justus

Tales of the Unearthly Northwest
Sojourn
"New Year's Eve in Conconully"
Reunion

Time in Yellowstone
Repeating History
True Gold
"Homesick"
Finding Home

Much Ado in Montana

Cross-Country: Adventures Alone Across America and Back

Made in the USA
Columbia, SC
15 November 2017